M000313382

# Creamy Bullets

*FICTION*

*by*

kevin sampsell

chiasmus press

PORTLAND

Chiasmus Press


www.chiasmuspress.com
press@chiasmusmedia.net

PRODUCED AND PRINTED IN THE UNITED STATES OF AMERICA

ISBN:   0-9815027-3-3

978-0-98150-273-1

cover concept:   Pete McCracken
cover design:   Matthew Warren
interior design:   Matthew Warren

# Praise for Kevin Sampsell's Previous Works:

"Not only do Kevin Sampsell's short stories have some of the most lively opening lines I've read since Donald Barthelme's; not only do they combine surreality with pathos; his stories also non-didactically offer important lessons for the attentive reader: **1.** On a first date with Satan, don't open your mouth too wide; **2.** Don't throw a sunflower at your girlfriend's head; **3.** Don't introduce your mother to the guy who's stalking you; **4.** Lost glove collecting is a hobby that leads to melancholy and vice versa. For a strange but somehow also incredibly useful education in contemporary American life, read his work."

—MATTHEW SHARPE,
author of *The Sleeping Father* and *Jamestown*

## Beautiful Blemish:

"Sampsell's prose ranges from taut to indifferent, bearing occasional whiffs of Charles Bukowski and Richard Brautigan, as well as Chris Ware and Dan Clowes, and his stories are full of horniness and wonder, morbid speculation and strange coincidence. For readers with tastes that range outside the mainstream, this is a gem of warmhearted idiosyncrasy and oddball observation."

–*Publishers Weekly*

"Sampsell is a master of the deadpan outrageous. His best stories hit two notes at once: funny and gross, creepy and sad, pathetic yet noble."

–*Willamette Week*

"So, I'm sitting here today. Kind of putting off writing again, and I'm reading Kevin Sampsell's new book called *Beautiful Blemish* and making all of these sounds out loud and alone. Loud laughing, but also those sort of shakes of the head where you just say, "Man..." and you sort of soak in exactly what it is Kevin Sampsell can do with words and, more amazingly, how he ALWAYS seems to do it."

–DAN KENNEDY,
author of *Rock On* and *Loser Goes First*

## A Common Pornography:

"Kevin Sampsell's stories are brief incantations, uppercuts to the gut, prose poems given over to the bloodiest realms of the self. It's all here: the emotional squalor, the sweet bite of loneliness. Make no mistake: Sampsell can write like hell."

–STEVE ALMOND,
author of *Not That You Asked*

"Beautiful and strange."

–*Geist Magazine*

# Acknowledgements:

Fresh Salmon in *Opium*

Girl Drummer (originally titled Drums)
   on *Minima*

Bubbles in *Stray Dog* and on *Sniffy Linings*

You and They on *Elimae*

This Old House on *Elimae*

What Great Tragedies in *LIT*

Stomach in *LIT*

Cold Cream on *Juked*

She Whispers, Nudges, Mumbles Something on
   *Word Riot*

Where Goal Posts Go to Die on *Monkeybycicle*
   (one sentence stories)

Ice Cream Bars on *Sniffy Linings*

Thirteen Mundane Dreams in *Mountain Man
   Dance Moves* (Vintage Books)

Trails in *Mitochondria* (Bullfight Media)

Don't Eat Paper in *Quick Fiction*

The Takeoff on *Pindeldyboz*

Big Cheese was written for a Family Dinner event
   at PICA's TBA festival in 2005 and was later
   published on *Pequin*

Sharon Calls in *LIT*, and on *Failbetter*

Not a Mermaid in *The Organ Review of Arts*,
   and on *Bullfight Review*

Writer's Block Theme Song in *The Penny
   Dreadful Review*

Jailbreaker in *Eye-Rhyme*

Monogamy on *5 Trope*

Fur Coat in *Fish Piss* (was originally written for a
    Lenny Bruce tribute night)
Flying Horses in *3rd Bed*
I Rest Between Them in *Yeti*
Headache in *Northwest Edge III: The End of Reality*
    (Chiasmus Press)
Outside of This Place on *Smokebox*
The Show in *2 girls review*
Swimsuit Issue in *The Empty Page: Stories Inspired
    by Sonic Youth* (Serpent's Tail)
Homewreckers in *Homewreckers: An Adultery
    Reader* (Soft Skull Press)
Krystal in *J&L Illustrated*
Layover (originally titled When He Found Me) in
    *The Unmade Bed* (Masquerade Books)
Today's Events on *Mud Luscious*
Reunion in *Night Train*
Jealousy is Policy in *Sniffy Linings 3* and on *Slouch*
Close Your Eyes on *Identity Theory* and in
    *Barcalounge*

NOTE FROM THE AUTHOR : I would like to thank all the editors who have helped shape these stories as well as my dear friends: Stephen Kurowski, Erika Geris, Jon Raymond, Barb Klansnic, Jackie Corley, Jen Joseph, Magdalen Powers, Mike Daily, Frank D'Andrea, Elizabeth Miller, Elizabeth Ellen, Melissa Lion, Gary Lutz, Michael Murphy, Andrew Monko, and so many others that would take up too many pages.

A special thanks to Pete McCracken (for the awesome cover), Jami Attenberg, Sam Lipsyte, Davy Rothbart, all the chiasmus crew (especially Lidia and Trevor), and my son Zach, who should wait at least five more years before reading some of these stories.

# CONTENTS

**small**

# Girl With Shaky Hands

"I thought that was a bird but it's a rollerskate," she said, looking at my shirt. Her fingernails looked clumpy, as if painted by a child. Her neck stuck out and her chin led her face. Her face seemed lost in my chest. "I don't suppose you like this cheese," she said. Her head popped back when she said this and she stuck something in her mouth. She chewed in an up-and-down manner and then in hard circles, like a strenuous exercise. She looked at me and waited. The music of the party, a mixed selection of music unfamiliar to the guests, made everyone feel insecure and dumb.

Someone screamed from the kitchen and I saw a flash or a spark out of the corner of my eye. "Emergency room!" someone shouted. A girl with a towel over her hand bustled toward me with a stunned white face. A man in a green angora sweater steered her toward the door. An older man with a beard followed them with something bobbing in a ziplock bag of ice. "We'll take my car," he shouted ahead of him.

Many people left after that. Someone said something about another party. A party with familiar music and some empty rooms for people who didn't like the small talk or fake socializing. The girl who asked about my shirt was on the front porch, smoking and crying. It was dark outside and the orange glow of her cigarette shook wildly in front of her face, like she was tracing a picture of something she couldn't focus on. I smelled the menthol smoke but I also smelled something else, more private and disturbing. I stood close by, wondering what to do next. "That could have been me," she said. She dropped the cigarette finally, and crushed its light.

# What Great Tragedies

She tried to explain to me how people always had throw up inside of them. It's there in your stomach too, she said, and poked me there. You just haven't thrown it up yet.

Everything we talked about was something I'd never talked about with anyone else. When she was eight, she went to the hospital twice. Once, she said, they tore a hole in my neck to get a fishhook out.

The other time was for a finger that was bit off by their pet parrot.

I looked at her neck, her fingers. I looked at her mouth as she spoke, her eyes—gray and calm. Maybe they were blue.

I was thrilled to be with her. This kind of love was lucky, I told myself. I actually did talk to myself about it sometimes, usually while driving, and then I would wonder if someone were hiding in the backseat.

—◁  *creamy bullets*

On the flipside though, I thought she must have been bored with me. What insights could I share? What great tragedies had I endured? I told her about the time when I rode a motorcycle into an empty ditch and then burnt my hand on the exhaust pipe pushing it off my leg. The lip sting I suffered at age twelve when a bee snuck into my orange soda can.

I wet my bed until I was thirteen. That was tough, I said.

See this ear, she finally said, as if waiting her turn. She pointed at her left ear. Sometimes it hears things opposite. Like you could say cold and I'll think you said hot.

I wasn't sure if she was kidding around. I usually had to wait a good beat or two to see how the silence played out. So I hate you is I love you? I asked.

Sometimes, she said. Yes. Sometimes, yes.

# Stomach

"I hate food," she said. She looked around the restaurant sadly, then picked up a plastic squirt bottle of sauce. "Have you tried this sauce, it's really good."

There was a lull in our conversation. She came to lunch heartbroken. We were longtime friends, but in this case, I wasn't helping. She tried again to explain. "It was just so perfect. It was the first time I'd been able to stay in the same room as someone else while I worked. He'd just lie in bed and wait. He was always ready."

The food came and I waited for her to take the first bite. She stuck the point of her knife in her burrito and cut a straight vertical line. It was a stomach, opened for surgery. She put a hand over her mouth. I watched her shoulders shake a little and then she dropped her hand. I wondered what it would be like to have meaningless sex with her.

She took a bite from the beany insides. "I don't feel any better," she sighed.

I couldn't look at her. I tried to say something but it came out ordinary and useless. She didn't seem to hear it though, or it didn't penetrate her despair. She had the look of a lost, confused animal. To make matters worse, the woman at the next table was wearing the same sweater.

I fiddled with my tacos, holding one with my right hand, at chest level.

I tried to eat without pleasure, for her sake.

# Fresh Salmon

The fresh salmon arrived Fed Ex. Jake and I would eat it that weekend after killing the coyote. We slept in the backyard wearing motorcycle helmets and garlic. Sally said she could smell our knees and she made us wear long johns. She watched over us from the back window as she made tartar sauce spiced with the eyes of the fish, from a recipe created by her suicidal father. He was scarred years ago when a coyote attacked him and toppled his fishing cooler. It's something in this family we can't bury fast enough.

# Girl Drummer

I used to stay out late and sometimes let a man earn a blowjob. I was loud and pretty and popular in certain abusive circles.

But there was that one time when I offended a friend of yours at a book signing. He was non-literary.

But now it seems I'm settling down. I get up early in the morning and eat healthy foods. I've even learned how to drive.

I would much rather go fishing in the quiet morning than fuck you in the basement on the broken chair next to the drum set.

# Bubbles

My elevator ride stops abruptly, between floors six and seven. A woman I've never seen before is in the elevator with me. I try to call an operator on the red telephone inside the emergency door but it only rings once before going mysteriously dead. "Can I see your wallet?" the woman asks me. After looking at the contents of my wallet, she hands it back and then looks through her purse. "Aha," she says, pulling out a pack of gum. "We may as well make the best of it," she tells me. She hands me a big cube of purple gum, the kind that junior high school girls chew. "You go first," she says. I chew vigorously and then push out a nicely-rounded bubble. She raises her eyebrows in approval. She chews slowly, her lovely lips curling, her jaw moving in a smooth little dance. Her bubble comes out confidently, without fear. It grows bigger like a puff of smoke. She pauses for

*creamy bullets*

a moment and says, "Mine's strawberry." It's bright red. She stares into my eyes. "What next?" I ask her. "Bubble fight," she says. We stand close without touching and press our gum together.

# You and They

One of the first things you do is figure out ways to shorten their name. As if you're trying to make your utterance of their name sound original in your own voice. Jacoline becomes Jackie becomes Jack becomes J. Dennis becomes Denny becomes Den becomes D.

And then you make your touch unique. You use just your fingers or your thumbs or your hands or your whole right arm when you touch. You clench. You breathe in sharply when you do this.

In the morning, you wrap your legs around them like seaweed. You run your fingers down their back and hear them make pleasing sounds. You see the lines, the scratches, blood under the skin. You press harder.

When they leave, you embrace by the door and pay attention to how you fit this way. Whose arms go where and where their face lands in your chest. If you feel the heartbeats, count them until you part. Measure them. Learn the rhythms.

# This Old House

Embarrassing ways to die: Getting hit in a crosswalk. Experimental aircraft crumpling into a tree. Dying in my sleep, not man enough to do it awake.

I wish you didn't watch over me like a hawk. Sitting behind me, clipping your toenails. Breathing your drunk wine breath. You're obsessed about cancer. About what causes it, how long you can live with it or suffer through it. About knowing people who have it. You seek them out and then say to me, I told you so. You make me feel your breasts for lumps. Your throat. Everywhere. I think about what's inside me too. If I look close enough I can see my own purple blood in my veins. When people change their bodies with the help of doctors and money, it reminds me of a house. Fixed up on the outside. Inside, it still looks like shit. I hold your hand in the dark. We talk about cancer in the dark. If I look at you I'll just see the outline of your hair. Is death like a song whose words are forgotten? Or is it the eight ball, scratched, falling into a hole, before the table is cleared?

# Cold Cream

He can't stop chewing his fingernails. He likes the grit inside. The chewy finger dirt. A blind date once told him it was bad for him. She said, "You're chewing on shit. That's actual shit." She was the same girl who later made him lick her fake leather boots. Then she got all prissy and wouldn't take her shirt off. He noticed that she had a dumb tattoo on her calf. They were making out on her couch while her roommate, a tall awkward girl with thick glasses, watched porn in her own room. Their wet mouth sounds were drowned out by the moaning television.

Every time he tried to paw at one of her buttons or zippers, she told him she looked better with clothes on. He told her he couldn't see anything anyway, with all the lights out. She said even his hands would like her better with her clothes on. He started to wonder

—◄ *creamy bullets*

if there was something wrong with her. Maybe she had a scar or a fake appendage.

Finally she said, "Okay. Wait," and he heard a zipper being pulled. Untoothing itself apart.

It was just her bag or purse.

He heard some unpacking of things and the ketchupy squirt of some lotion. "Let it out," she said to him.

He felt her hand move toward him then, something cold poking him in the stomach and moving down. There was so much of it in her hand, he could barely feel her fingers. They felt like cold breakfast sausages.

When she was done with him, she gave him a wad of toilet paper to clean up. A bunch of it stuck to him. His penis looked like a papier-mâché puppet.

"Can I do it to you?" he asked.

"Not today," she said.

It really bothered him that she said Not today instead of Not tonight. It sounded snide the way she said it. Like thanks, but no thanks.

He didn't know what to do with himself. He felt a deep connection to the couch.

He thought he heard her laugh. But maybe it was coming from her roommate's room.

# Remembering Her

Her name was a small town name, an unusual name...a long, dark, spiraling name.

A boy's name from another country.

Her name was said by others over baskets of chips. It was the name of a mermaid or a mermaid's pet when they're lost—posters on telephone poles...a lost name, a wanted name.

Her name was like mine without all the breathing.

In the dark it was like a clock radio that wakes me up too early wondering what her name is.

What did it smell like?

How do you spell it?

# Where Goal Posts Go to Die

I went onto the field where they were tearing the goal posts down and several people were stuffing the various parts under their arms and carrying them out to their cars (right crossbar, left crossbar, the actual net where the football lands) and I asked one of them what they were planning on doing with the goal posts but he was interrupted by a fan of the other team sulking away and spitting into the astroturf, "If our fucking kicker wasn't a shitheel, we would have stole the game," and I wondered if that was the right word: stole, stolen, stealed—I wasn't really sure because sometimes in the excitement of post-game goal post tearing down, I lose track of grammar, of the way words change with time and tense and as I was getting into my car to drive away two men tapped me on the shoulder and I noticed that they were both exactly twenty-five pounds overweight (as if they each stuffed a bag of dog food down their sweats) and they held out part of the lower crossbar, asking if I had room in my trunk for it and saying they needed a ride out to the beach because that's where everyone was going and that's where the goal posts would be buried and that's where we would drink more beer and that's where we would sing into the wind and that's where we would wait for something to bloom and grow further.

# Ice Cream Bars

I am fashionably depressed in the window of a small cafe. An old woman rolling a shopping cart down the sidewalk sees me and steps inside. She opens a large dirty bag and takes out some pots and pans. She finds a quart of ice cream somewhere at the bottom and tells me how to make ice cream bars. One of the pans is full of fresh brownies and she takes a spatula in her left hand. "Make sure the ice cream is softened," she says. She dips the spatula into the ice cream and smears some on top of the brownies like frosting. She graciously hands me the spatula. Spreading the thawing ice cream feels good.

The cute girl that works in the cafe puts on a cassette of happy Irish music.

"You must have some good French chocolate," the old woman continues. She takes out a colorful tin can adorned with a strange word and opens it with a can opener. She pours the chocolate over the top of the ice cream. "Now, we must go to your house and put them in the freezer," she says.

For the next few days, the lady lives with me and I evaluate my life. I make a list of things that make me happy. I make a list of things that make me sad. The old lady reads each list and responds accordingly. One night I draw a bath for her and decorate the surface of the water with small flowers from the garden.

Later, we go out to find a new place to eat dinner. She bends her short arm into the crook of my arm. We walk together and for some reason I feel like an actor, taking his mother to the Academy Awards. Lights are popping, people are smiling. Our picture will be in *People* magazine.

On the day she disappeared from my life I went back to the cafe and sat gloating in the window.

The cute girl came out from behind the counter and sat beside me. The music was low as she touched my hand and asked where my mother was.

# Thirteen Mundane Dreams

**1.** You were in the laundry room and I walked in. You asked me what I wanted.

**2.** My mom was trying to grind some coffee beans but it wouldn't work. Then she realized the grinder wasn't plugged in.

**3.** My grandfather was fishing at that really popular lake outside of town. I drove up in a Ford Taurus and asked if he needed a ride home. He got in the car and farted.

**4.** I was watching TV in the front room when the mail arrived. I looked at it sitting there on the floor. A Domino's Pizza ad and the cable bill.

**5.** My cat walked into the bedroom like he was going to make an announcement. I watched him for a couple minutes before I realized he couldn't talk, because he's a cat.

**6.** I was at a Moby concert. He was fiddling with a keyboard and there were gospel singers shouting something over and over.

**7.** You were watching TV and I walked in and showed you the cable bill. I was wearing that hat I always wear.

**8.** This guy I work with called and asked me if I could come into work for him. I started to say yes but then he said he was feeling better and that he'd see me later.

**9.** I was reading this old biography of Gerald Ford when my neighbor knocked on the door. I answered it and he gave me back the hedge clippers I let him borrow.

**10.** You and I were at a funeral home. We walked over to a coffin and it was empty. The price tag next to it said 50% off.

**11.** My friend Matt was sitting on a ledge eating his lunch. At first I thought he was on a high building or bridge, but it was just a Safeway loading dock. He jumped off and walked away.

**12.** You were at a hockey game and that guy you slept with eight years ago was sitting a few rows away from you, closer to the ice. He looked the same, but maybe eight years older.

**13.** I woke up with a headache. You told me to take some aspirin and fell back asleep.

# Racial

She jutted out her chest in hopes of communicating something inside her. She held wobbly onto her small red clutch while staring at the man in the seat across from her. A thought crawled across the bottom of her mind: racial joke...racial joke...racial joke...

Her feet were sticky and wedged, pointing at everyone through sloppy black plastic pumps.

This streetcar is not a car and this is hardly a street, she thought to herself, sure that there were others who were thinking the same thing. The sounds of sighs and people singing inside their throats gained momentum as she slacked against the noise. She listened for bad words in the air and felt eager, herself, to say something wrong.

# She Whispers, Nudges, Mumbles Something

She felt like she was getting sick when the bass kicked in. It was the low, crunchy, beneath-your-feet kind of buzz. She moved away from the blast of the speaker. A tall, broad-shouldered man in an orange hunting jacket was her shield. She held on to him for security. He squirmed as if surprised but he shouldn't have been surprised. He knew she was looking at him. That she was easy and bored and changed her hairstyle all the time because of this boredom.

This was a dirty band they listened to. They had a song called Republican Bathhouse. They had two bass players, two keyboard players, clothes that were terrible in all the right ways. They crossed lines and expected people to follow.

The man in the hunting jacket turned around and said something to her but there was no hope in hearing the words. She held him tight for an amount of time that didn't seem too long or desperate or bold. Her grip loosened and by the end of the show she had a single finger hooked into the belt loop on the back of his jeans. She pulled on the jeans playfully and looked at his ugly underwear. She had the urge to let a drop of spit out, to watch it roll down his spine, into the gutter of his ass. Instead she blew on his peach fuzz there. She imagined a field of dead grass blowing in the wind.

They walked out to his car with their ears buzzing. Everything sounded like it was muffled by a pillow—their footsteps, people talking, cars backing up on the gravel. She let go of his belt loop and walked to the passenger side of his car. She looked over the top of the car and saw him standing there. He seemed shocked, as if noticing her for the first time. He accidentally smiled at her before getting in. He paused after putting his seat belt on and then leaned over and unlocked the passenger door.

She got in and didn't put her seat belt on. He started the car and the stereo was playing a CD by the band they just saw. It seemed like too much. She told herself that she wouldn't want to listen to this band again for a while. She felt like she just endured something.

He turned down the radio and looked embarrassed. He said something that she didn't quite catch but it sounded like, "I live with my mom."

"That's okay," she said. She pushed a button for the electric windows. It went down halfway.

"I like your hair that way," he said.

She looked at him sharply when he said this. She mumbled something to herself so he couldn't hear her. She knew that the ringing of his ears was probably to her advantage. So she kept mumbling and whispering and smiling at him. She liked that simply playing with the volume of her voice made her words like a foreign language that he struggled to understand, grasping only fragments. He was too polite to ask her to repeat herself. She whispered, "I live with my mom too" and looked sad. She smiled again quickly, poked his side with her elbow, and said a bit louder, "But she's deaf, so she won't hear us."

He laughed and said, "I know. I'm totally deaf right now!" He put his hand on her knee and said, as if making a rule, "Let's not talk any more tonight."

She pointed him to her home. The buzzing between the two of them turned to silence and the cool, quiet sensation of everything else began to overtake them.

# Trails

The manager owned a goldfish that had begun to grow hair. The girl saw it one day, making waves into trails on the surface of its tank. What's wrong with Teller, asked the girl of the manager.

Penn died, he replied. He walked over to where she crouched, looking in on the fish. He flicked his cigarette ash into the water. Cancer, he said. She looked at him hard. It spreads, he coughed.

Why is he growing hair, she asked more specifically this time.

It's his way of telling us to fuck off, he said.

# Don't Eat Paper

My son was getting ready to eat dinner when he ran to the bathroom, doubling over with stomach grief. I put his pasta down and went to see what the matter was. He threw up some of his root beer, some of his elementary school hot lunch.

He always preferred the sink instead of the toilet when vomiting. I stood behind him and put my hand on his back for support.

"I didn't know you were feeling sick. Do you have a fever?" I ran the water in the sink, trying to keep the smell from sticking.

"Don't eat paper," he said, before bending over the sink again.

I pushed lightly on his stomach and wondered how paper might break down in there. How it might come out. I remembered how it felt to throw up as a kid and how my father would hold my stomach for support. I pressed for details.

"Did someone make you do that?"

"No. I just did it."

I tried to think of why someone would eat paper.

"Was it a secret message?"

"Yes."

"Who gave it to you?"

He didn't answer, choking forth more bile. I figured it would be a good lesson for him. When you throw up something as a child you never want that thing in your mouth for the rest of your days. I remember once getting sick on Lorna Doone shortbread cookies. I never touched them again. As an adult though, people throw up all the time but always return, steely and unshaken, to the cause: beer, corndogs, sushi.

I fumbled for more information.

"How much paper was it?"

He turned on the water, rinsed some thickened spit down the drain.

"It was just a little piece of notebook paper. With the little holes down the side."

"Was it from a girl?" I asked for some unknown reason.

He wretched loudly and some chunks of food came out. I made a mental checklist before I washed them down: raisins, fruit roll-ups, maybe some tuna fish.

But also: a raggedy flag shape of paper, about three inches in length. I pinned it to the porcelain as the rest swirled away. My son fell back against the wall, exhausted and pale, breathing like a runner at the end of a marathon. "There," he said. "I think that's it."

I tore the paper as I tried to smooth it out but I could still read it. In evil-looking block letters it said: DON'T EAT PAPER.

# The Takeoff

I get excited just by sitting next to you. I spread the small blanket over my lap so that no one can tell. This is the third airplane we've been on today. We are preparing for takeoff. I've got the window seat and you're in the middle. Next to you, in the aisle seat, is a sixty-year old woman knitting something.

As the flight attendants vapidly show us how to tighten our seatbelts and deploy the oxygen masks, I guide your hand under the blanket. You move your fingers there. By taking sharp inhaling breaths, I can make my penis hop. It's like a stupid pet trick. It makes you smile.

Just as your fingers start to trace my zipper, a male attendant walks up and starts talking to the lady next to you about her knitting. She tells him that she's making a frock and for some reason I can't

*creamy bullets*

quite remember what a frock is. Is it like a poncho? An apron? The attendant lingers a little and I catch his eyes drifting away from the frock and focusing on our blanket. We are sitting very still and you even have your eyes closed, feigning sleep, though underneath the blanket my zipper is down and you are prying that part of me out.

"I couldn't work on something like that," the attendant says. "I don't have the patience."

I look over at the lady's hands. They quickly and smoothly work the black yarn and red needles. I wonder if knitting is like hand exercise, if it helps to thwart arthritis. Her skin does look young, soft, made of pearl. She has a rhythm going like a drummer. The attendant walks away. The plane is starting to rumble down the runway. I look up at the lady's face and she looks angry now.

Under the blanket, your hand is gripping me, moving slowly. I shift toward you so the movement isn't noticeable. We are up in the air.

"Would you like some gum?" the woman is suddenly asking us. I look up and see her chewing excitedly on her own piece. She is looking right at me and I notice that she has a very loose neck. It wiggles as we gain altitude. "It helps you from popping your ears," she says.

"No, thanks," I say.

"I'll take some," you say, your eyes snapping open. You let go of me and take your hand from under the blanket. You take the gum and unwrap it. It's a flat pink slab. I watch you put it in your mouth. I wait for your hand to return. It does, feeling cold for a second. "Thanks," you say to the woman.

The woman just nods and chews, a smile on her face as she concentrates on her needlework. I focus on it as well—the looping, the weaving, the clicking of the needle points. I'm starting to relax when the pressure comes. Your hand is putting me away as my ears pop.

# medium

# Big Cheese

My dad owned a fondue restaurant when I was younger. It was called Big Cheese. Everyone had to wear those fake cheeseheads like Green Bay Packers fans. Even the cooks and dishwashers. I started out as a dishwasher but was promoted to server on my 17th birthday. I liked the job because I made tips and would always go out and spend them on paisley clothes on the weekend. I loved paisley for some reason.

The restaurant was always struggling before I started working there. But then, for some reason, things picked up. There was actually word-of-mouth happening—and this was in an oppressed factory town where no one said a thing to anyone. You were lucky to get a smile at the barbershop.

I started to think this buzz was due to my father's frequent trips to Nova Scotia, where he would personally buy huge boxes of exotic cheese to be delivered to the restaurant. "This is the key to our new life," he told me, caressing a forty-pound block of waxed something. "This shit is the motherfucking key!"

This was around the time he started swearing and yelling a lot and wearing rings on all his fingers.

It was around Christmas of that year when I realized something different was going on at Big Cheese.

One family ordered a fondue pot full of something called Nordic Swiss Calcutta. We served our pots of cheese with bread sticks, vegetables, sausages, or any variety of dipping foods. The mother and father of this family quickly commandeered the Calcutta and instructed me to bring out a different kind for their pimply twin girls. "Something less intense," the parents laughed. I brought out the Smoked Hickory Feta for the girls and they all seemed satisfied. The father started whispering something to the mother. The girls poked their sticks of bread into the murky pot and lifted them out, sloppy blobs bit by teeth and smeared with cheap lipstick. I stayed in the kitchen for a few minutes, talking to Joey, the headbanger cook, and watching the dining room from a safe distance.

"Judas Priest is the greatest," Joey told me. "You wanna borrow their tape?"

"Sure," I said. I was distracted and bored and trying to concoct some fantasy involving the twin girls that I could use later when I got home, or maybe when I had to eventually go to the walk-in freezer.

"They're the Beatles of this generation," Joey said. "The Beatles in leather, dude."

I forgot what he was even talking about. I went out to check on the family of four. The father was still whispering to his wife. As I got closer though, I realized he was sticking his tongue in her ear. She had her eyes half-closed, fully enjoying it. I saw a spackle of cheese congealing on her chin. "Go out and play," the father told the girls. His left hand lifted to his wife's chest and began clawing aggressively there. The girls were glad to be excused. They too were suddenly alive and boiling with passion. They bolted through the front door and threw themselves into a pile of snow. I heard one of them say, "Pretend I'm Jesus."

My dad had me come to his office the next day. He wanted to give me the "fingerfucking lowdown" as he called it.

He pulled out a map and dramatically crumpled it into a ball. He threw it in the tin wastebasket and threw a lit match in. Nothing happened. He tried again. I wasn't sure what he was doing. "Hold a goddamn second," he told me, and exited the office. He came back five minutes later with a can of lighter fluid. He took off his dress shirt, flexing his tank-topped form, and doused the shirt with the smelly liquid. He lit it on fire and threw it in the trash with the map. "Nova fucking Scotia," he said. He looked at me hard.

"I d-don't understand," I stammered.

His skin flushed red and he shouted, "Daddy's a drug dealer!" His ringed hand formed a fist and he pounded the top of his heavy oak desk. "Most of the cheese we serve to the customers is from downtown Cleveland, but do you think I can say that to Mr. Nigel Restaurant Reviewer? Hell no! They come to our place to escape. They want to think of Nova Scotia or cranberry manchego puree or hazelnut German cheddar or some other shit like that. Do you know where those names come from? My frickin' hat! I write down a bunch of fluffy words and let my blind hands create a menu. But it's the damn magic mushrooms that make people come back for more."

I rubbed my eyes, thinking for a moment that I was dreaming. The flames were still going in the trash. "Are the mushrooms from Nova Scotia?" I asked.

"Jesus, no!" he spat. "And it's not just mushrooms. It's cocaine, marijuana, and some new stuff called Prozac." Finally, he stuck his leg in the garbage and started stomping out the fire. Ashes and smoke billowed around him like the devil.

I stepped back, found the door, stumbled out, eyes watering and brain hurting. I was never the same after that day. I knew dad's thinly-veiled drug empire would be found out soon. He was losing his cool and I don't think he even knew where Nova Scotia was.

My innocence was squashed that day. Melted, as if in a pot full of cheese. Never to return. Never fucking ever.

# Sharon Calls

I'd hear from Sharon once every couple years, on a pay phone, in some state-sponsored home. I imagined other folks her age squirming around her in wheelchairs. Bad art on the walls. Plants dying in plastic pots on high windowsills.

We were never really friends but I was nice to her when others weren't, so she kept in touch. Her most recent call was a week ago, as I was sitting down to dinner with my family. She was at a new home. She called it "the prison."

I asked her if she was allowed to leave.

"Oh, sure," she said. "But this place is out in the boonies and I don't have any teeth."

"What happened to your teeth?"

"I had an accident and they won't give me replacements."

Sharon was a poet I knew from the days I used to go to open mic poetry readings, about ten years ago. Even then, her body and mind were decaying. But she was a good poet and her craziness was vicariously thrilling to most people, if not a little confrontational. She walked with a cane, and never drove a car. Before moving to Portland in her late 30s, she was a regular in the San Francisco poetry scene and had a couple books published. One of her author photos told me that she used to be a bombshell. High cheekbones, sex kitten eyes, and blonde hair slicked back like a model.

Sometimes she heckled other poets.

"Did you hear that?" she asked me. "People are always yelling here. Even at bedtime."

I did hear something through the phone line. Like she was calling from a carnival all of the sudden. I asked her if she was able to do any writing.

"They threw away my computer. I have to write in my journal. I have lots of journals. But they're not publishable."

I wondered when Sharon was last published. I used to see her work in several small magazines but that was many years ago. I was never clear on what was physically wrong with her. She once said something about Agent Orange. She was married to someone who was exposed to Agent Orange and it affected her too. I don't know anything about war chemicals. And I'm not sure if she was ever telling the truth.

Someone told me her brain was damaged from a bad drug prescription. Someone else implied that she was beat up when she was a stripper in San Francisco. Before she was a stripper she taught sex education to high schoolers. Her friends back then were mostly Scientologists. L. Ron Hubbard wannabes. She was reckless and intimate with many of them. She turned her past into poems. She also talked about— and wrote about—how much she hated her father. She called him "The Devil." Now she had different enemies. New enemies, all the time.

"There's a guy down the hall from me who steals peoples' cats," she told me. "He takes them to the boiler room and then they're gone. He broke into my room and took my black wig. I've called the police on him several times but I can't press charges because I'm in their system and they don't believe me."

"What do you mean, 'in their system'?"

"The police have been told not to take my calls."

I understood that what she was saying was the truth to her. She wasn't exaggerating. If she broke into police files and looked up her name she would be shocked if they didn't corroborate what she was telling me.

"Are you still writing?" she asked me.

"Not poetry," I told her. "Mostly short stories."

"That's what I should do," she said. "That's where the money is." There was a pause while she waited for me to respond but I didn't know what to say.

"Are you friends with Butch Stein?" she asked me.

"I know who he is," I answered. Butch was a guy who won a bunch of poetry slams but would sometimes disappear on long drug binges. He once called me to apologize for something I couldn't remember. He had to, he told me. It was one of the twelve steps. To make amends. Straight from the AA Big Book, written over fifty years ago.

"He tried to fuck me," Sharon said.

There was a stunned pause. For a second, I forgot whom I was talking to. I tried to piece it together. Butch, a handsome twenty-nine year old with an Irish accent and Sharon, a fifty year old head case with a body twice its age. "What? Butch Stein?"

"Oh, you bet. He gave me a ride home about a year ago and tried to get fresh on my couch. He didn't expect me to put up a fight, but I did."

"That's really weird," I said before realizing she may take that as a slight. "I mean, doesn't he have a girlfriend or something?"

"Some people like to fuck cripples," she snorted. "I'm not interested in sex anymore. Or I should say that I *am* interested in sex, just not sex with penises."

"I understand," I told her for some reason. I heard someone else yelling in the background where Sharon was. Again I imagined a group of slouching wheelchair drivers rolling aimlessly around her, one of them squawking about their medicine or a baseball game.

"I guess I better go," she said. "I just wanted to see if you remembered me. Sometimes I see your name somewhere and I remember that you weren't as full of shit as some other people. Remember when you bought groceries for me?"

I thought about it for a second and did remember. Maybe six years ago. She gave me a list over the phone. All frozen foods and toilet paper. I had to take them to her in her fifth floor apartment. It was a bland place with brown carpet in the hallways and clammy air full of TV-through-the-wall noises. Her dishes hadn't been washed and I think she complained about me getting the wrong brand of ice cream. "I remember," I said.

"Okay. Talk to you later." She hung up before I could say anything else. I suddenly felt dazed, and then, strangely, I thought of numerous other things I could have talked to her about. My family had started dinner without me. I held the phone away from my ear and let the dial tone hum freely.

In my head, I saw a clear picture of the phone that was just on the other end. It was a plastic green one, hanging on the wall, push buttons nearly rubbed clean, a small crack splitting the bottom where someone once punched it. A sticker with emergency numbers, applied on the side, top left corner of it peeling away, ink smudged. A metal phone book holder coming out of the wall underneath, empty and cold.

# Today's Events

## — DEFENSE —

I'm at my son's lacrosse practice. It's on a big soccer field and the sun beats down. I'm watching from a distance, under a tree, in the shade. I didn't bring a lawn chair, so I sit uncomfortably on the grass. The kids are grouped into teams and my son plays in one scrimmage, about thirty yards to my right. They wear helmets but no pads. My son stands in the middle of the field as the other kids race around him trying to cradle the orange ball. His holds his stick high in the air, like he's waiting for a pass.

I call him over after the other team scores a goal. I tell him to get more involved, to chase after the ball, play defense.

He goes back and starts paying more attention. His defense is aggressive. He stick-checks a player for the other team and the ball bounces loose. The kid seems surprised, calls out to him, "This is just a friendly game!"

After the practice, I wait in the shade as my son gets a drink of water. There is a crow nearby, standing alone. I look at him and say out loud, "Crow." I stare at him for a while expecting something from him. I'm not sure what. Perhaps I want him to say, "Human."

— SLURPEE —

We go to 7-11 to get a money order and an after-practice Slurpee. I start to pull into a parking spot, but there is a truck with its driver's door open. I wait for the person to notice but they're too busy doing something. I want to honk but instead I move my car slightly to the left, barely fitting into the space. I look over and see that the woman in the truck is leaning over and looking for something in the glove box of the truck. Her knees are on the driver's seat and she is wearing a short skirt. I can see almost her entire ass. It doesn't look like she is wearing any underwear. I can't tell how old she is. She could be sixteen or she could be forty. There is a yellow and blue bruise just below her left ass cheek. I look in the backseat and see my son playing his Gameboy, oblivious to the woman. We go inside and I feed money into the money order machine. $189.75. My son is helping himself at the Slurpee machine.

The woman comes into the store, walking with heavy steps. Her face looks haggard and she is wearing cheap-looking rings on her hands. Her face is much older than her body. I see her buy something in a box but I can't tell what it is. Cat food or cereal maybe.

When my son and I leave the store, I see the woman sitting in her truck. She's looking around nervously. We get in the car and my son holds the Slurpee to his head. I have to go back into the store to borrow a pen for my money order. I write out the info on my money order as the clerk watches me. When I go back outside, I see the woman yelling something and hitting her steering wheel. Her sounds though, are trapped inside the truck with her.

— DINNER —

At home, I get ready to make dinner. I turn on the oven and spread frozen French fries onto a cooking sheet. When I open the oven door, I notice the smell of throw up. I wonder if someone threw up in the oven. I imagine what it would be like to throw up in the oven.

The air outside is cooling down as the sun lowers. It's still too hot though.

I spread the French fries so they're not touching, like the instructions say. I open the door to the oven. It makes a loud creaking noise. I throw up in the oven.

# Not a Mermaid

It was some lake up in Washington. Some boat just big enough for the both of us. Some green water smell. Some time apart from your family. I put your hand in that private spot and you responded by doing the same with my hand. The water underneath us rocked just slightly, so we didn't have to move our bodies to enjoy the contact. Your mother and father were inside a cabin somewhere, preparing lunch. They would never know that we did such things in the boat. Look, you said, and pointed to a huge fish swimming underneath us, just discernible enough for us to see. It looked blue and silver and strong.

It looks like a shark, you said.

It's not a shark, I replied. But still I was scared just because of the thing's size.

Do you think it's a piranha?

Don't be silly.

It's something big.

We watched it move below us, gleaming in the sun and coming more into focus as we watched.

When we arrived back at the cabin there was something unsettled between us. We sat on the couch but didn't hold hands. You had that far away look, as if you were still thinking about the fish. I hope we don't have fish for dinner, you said.

In our sleeping bags later, you insisted on sleeping with your head pointing away from the water. I wanted to sleep the other way so I could look at the stars through the unzipped sky flap of our tent. Go ahead, you said. Tell me what you see.

I scanned the stars for shapes. Look, I said, there's a bunch over here shaped like a Christmas tree.

You're just saying that, you mumbled.

That night I had the dream about the fish. He came out of the water and walked up to the tent. In this dream, I watched his shadow walking with a limp and I wanted to scream. When he leaned down to talk to me he said, Don't get your hopes up. I'm not a mermaid.

He held out a part of his body that looked almost like a hand. That's when I felt that wetness, not in real life of course, but in dream life. I shook his "hand" and we talked for what felt to be a long time. He said he knew what I was doing in the boat and

I better watch it. When he saw the sun starting to emerge he said he had to leave. He tried to embrace me and I felt some other kind of wetness from him as we touched. Maybe tears.

Did I do something wrong, you said as I woke up. You were out of your sleeping bag and pressing against mine, your arm across my chest. You were crying. You always cried in the morning for some reason.

You look so mad, you said.

What do you mean, I asked.

Your forehead is all scrunched up, like you're troubled. She rubbed her palm on my brow as if to smooth it out.

I was asleep, I said. I can't control what I do when I'm sleeping.

# Writer's Block Theme Song

Her small house is made with bricks. In the front room everything is of equal importance. Every object, pumping with electricity. Her computer is staring at her. Her television is on but the volume is low. Her clocks drone away and her books are left open, hanging in mid-sentence. She knows that if she doesn't go to bed soon she will be up until the morning and then she will have to sleep all day. She thinks about the effect this will have on her later in the week.

When she was a man she would sleep all the time and that is why she is a woman now. If she goes to bed now she will be able to wake up at a decent hour and then turn on all her things again.

She struggles with loneliness. You don't need to be told that. Just look at her, sitting there. She glances at the television from time to time, hoping that something grabs her attention, and when something finally does she feels empty inside.

The world is so big, she thinks. It seems to keep expanding the more and more she stays inside. She feels insignificant if she can't write, if she can't fill her computer screen with words.

When she is able to write, the world becomes smaller with each word, each page. Her chair fits her body better, her legs, her back, her skin, all of her that is not male. But only sometimes.

Her suspicious history contains these facts: She has written one hundred poems and kept eight or nine of them. She once wrote a 200-page book that was published by a university press. It was about airplane catastrophes. That was eight years ago, when she first became a woman. She wrote the book when she was a man but couldn't get it published. She wonders now what captivated her to write such a book. She had a brief stint at a bad local magazine as an assistant editor. She quit because she heard someone making fun of the magazine at a restaurant. The people at her neighborhood bookstore keep forgetting her name.

She goes into the kitchen. Her freezer is full of food that keeps falling out on her toes. She makes toast with peanut butter. She eats all of it except the top crust. She puts music on the stereo and puts the television on mute. She picks up a book and reads half of a page. She decides to let the music put her to sleep and try again tomorrow.

# Jailbreaker

I know everything there is to know about getting into jail. Trust me. This is going to hurt me more than it hurts me.

It started with the parking citation. I just went into the store for a second. A loaf of bread and one of those new Snickers bars. Five seconds tops. When I get back out the ink is still wet on the ticket as it flaps under my windshield wiper. I look around and spot the bastard getting into his parking enforcement buggy. The kind that looks like a fucking golfing cart gave birth to a dwarf. It's got three wheels and a sign that says DO NOT FOLLOW, like you'd ever want to. He sees me coming and tries to get away by making a right turn at the corner. I get a good running start and drill him like vintage Lawrence Taylor. Piece of shit flips over like a bike messenger. I kick his midget wheels and smash his little walkie talkie. Then I go to jail.

They dress me up in some orange jumpsuit and trot me out in front of the judge so he can stare at me over his bifocals and mutter some law school psychobabble.

They let me call my cousin Randy before they throw me in the cell. Randy's not there so I try to leave a message before getting cut off. Piece of shit machine. He thinks he saves twenty bucks a month with that thing. Only assholes think shit like that.

When I get to see my view behind the bars at the Strom Thurmond Correctional Prison, I make the acquaintance of my cellmate, a wannabe rapper named Derelikt. He's up in my grill about his hood and how I'm not welcome to buy a Hostess Fruit Pie at his Uncle's convenient store. His orange gear has been modified to look a little more street and he's got a head band holding back this crazy 'fro that's about a foot high and has so much product in it I'm afraid it'd blow up if I so much as burp. I tell him that I can do fifty push-ups and can bench press twice his weight.

He's swaying back and forth right in front of me, rapping: I won't hesitate/if you get me irate/(indecipherable) dinner plates/until you learn to navigate/(indecipherable) gay or straight/I'll make you my playmate...

*— creamy bullets*

I don't understand half of it but I know it's not nice, so I knock him over and accidentally bang his head against the metal toilet. He scrambles to his feet and I push him again. He hits the toilet again. This goes on for a while and he keeps hitting the lip of the shitter and getting worse by the minute. Eventually he dies. Then I go to jail.

I'm in the lunchroom at the Jeb Bush Correctional Prison when a posse of slackjawed hillbillies tries to cut me open like a watermelon. I swiftly sidestep them and then disarm them with a series of kicks and thrown biscuits, wet with gravy. They're such a sad lot, they make me look like Jackie Chan. One dude deflects a dry biscuit off his rubbery chicken neck and convulses on the ground until his heart stops. Then I go to jail.

Out in the exercise yard of the Pete Wilson Correctional Prison, I'm walking the circle and listening to the *woosh* of the nearby ocean over the high walls. I tried to climb the east wall last week but the cyclone barbed wire proved too tricky, even with a pair of stolen oven mitts. This place ain't so bad though. You can sit in your cell and listen to the waves and the birds outside and it gets kind of peaceful. As I walk, I start to hear a little buzzing sound. I look down and see a tiny remote control car make its way to me. No one else is outside. I reach down and pick up the toy. There's a note attached. It's telling me to come over to a red Port-a-Potty that I've never seen before.

When I get over there I swear I hear a voice. A woman's voice. I cautiously open the door but don't see anyone. In here, the voice says.

I look into the pot and witness the face of the most beautiful woman I have ever seen. She's smiling and motioning to me to come in with her. I sniffed the air in there first to see if it smelled bad but it didn't. It just smelled like strong seawater, like the beach.

Take off your shoes, she says. Those fuckers will sink ya'.

I took off my shoes and even stripped down to my underwear for good measure. When I'm all the way inside (had to pop my shoulder out of its socket for a minute), she turns her back toward me and asks me to obliterate this huge pimple. I squeeze and squeeze and she screams and starts to sweat a little. We fall in love and spend the rest of the week having sex on a nearby island. We're married in a quick private ceremony performed by the local voodoo priestess. Before our honeymoon, my new wife takes me to a big department store to buy some silk sheets. While I'm in the home entertainment section, I see my mug shot on about fifty screens. The colors are a little off on a bunch of them and my skin looks green or brownish. My face all over the place, sick-looking. Some security guy spots me and takes out his taser. He's trying to be sneaky, coming up from behind, but I see his reflection in one of the TV screens, right next to my own reflection, which sits mask-like on top of my televised face. I quickly pretend like I'm looking at some computer equipment. When he's about to zap me, I spin around and swing a computer mouse in his face. It works like you'd expect, quick and stealth. I can't help myself though and I start shouting and yipping and swinging the mouse around my head like a lasso. A sales clerk acts fast and comes at me with a box cutter. He is able to dodge my swinging mouse attack and cut me deep in the belly. The medics come and grant me thirty-two stitches and a couple of staples. Then I go to jail.

At the Captain Vere Correctional Prison, I spend most of my time writing letters to my wife. I know her name is Kathey (or Cathey) but I haven't learned how to spell it yet. I'm not sure what letter it starts with so I decide to call her "Athey".

Athey has a cousin whose boyfriend's stepfather has a twin brother that works for the security company that makes the keys for the prison. She uses her connections and delivers me a concealed key on one of her conjugal visits. I am able to retrieve it during an inspired session of oral sex. She even put it in a little pink envelope with my name on it. We plan to meet outside in the nearby Costco parking lot the following evening.

The next morning at breakfast, I tell all the lifers that I'm good as out. Lifers don't give a rat's crap. They're in for good. I tell them I'll get one of their wives to pull the same trick but most of them are gay now and won't go down on a woman. Still, I give myself a tattoo to show loyalty to my prison brethren; a heart with a ball and chain around it.

When I find Athey's rusted-out Honda Civic the next day, she is asleep, with an opened Family Size bag of Dorito's in the passenger seat. I wake her up with a key tap on her window. We embrace quickly and make for the exit. Once on the freeway, we are chased by helicopters and state troopers. We run over a strip of spikes and spin wildly into the concrete median. We flip over the barrier into opposing traffic and smash into a semi, which straightens us out. We continue to drive on our tire rims and find the nearest exit, where we lose our pursuit on a rural road somewhere in the dark. Unfortunately, we run out of gas and have to hike across a dirt field. Out of nowhere, we're hit with spotlights and chopper blades are blowing dirt in our eyes. "Freeze!" someone yells.

The way the cops are talking I realize they were tipped off. Goddamn stepfather's twin cousin!

In the back of the squad car, Athey and I stretch our arms from behind our backs. We hold hands and I realize I've lost my ring. Then I go to jail.

I do a lot of thinking at the Julius Caeser Correctional Prison. I think about love and second chances and practicing yoga and the Denver Broncos' playoff run. There are many things important to think about at this point of my life.

This is the toughest prison I've ever been in and I even have a job, like I'm going to be here for a while or something. I'm in charge of popcorn and refreshments. That's right. You heard me. I have to make sure the kernels don't get burnt in the popper before we start the movies on Friday nights. I've been contemplating making a device that'll utilize the hot oil as a burning chemical weapon, but they watch you real good here. And there are cameras. So I just hand out little paper bowls of popcorn and pour the flat generic cola in the cups. Last night we watched *Rain Man*. I like the part where Dustin Hoffman freaks out when Tom Cruise tries to get him on the airplane. I think I'll do that next time they try to get me in jail. I'll start to screech in a high voice and recoil and figure out some crazy math in my head.

Yeah, someday I'll do that. I'll be like that guy. The cops will get embarrassed and start looking around and people will wonder what they're doing to me, they'll point and say something like, *What are they doing to that poor man?* And the handcuffs will be put away. And the pepper spray will be reholstered. And I won't have to come here anymore. Then you can stop listening to my problems.

# Monogamy

I know you're going to nibble the guy down the hall...at just this moment your eyes have the same look as the night you told me...I was hungry and then I wasn't...you went ahead and ordered and I watched you eat...is it good?

I think I made the decision as I moved you into the new apartment...I was going to trust you as much as you trusted me...you can't even lift me to throw me.

You said: Forget about it.
You said: He's gross.
You said: I hate people with red hair.

You would bite me and later we would eat breakfast... I don't like my stomach feeling this way...everyone seems to yell at me everyday all the time now...I should be mad at you.

You said:  Not down the hall, on the third floor.

Your window looks out onto Broadway...or is it his window?...it was that night after he worked late at the Texaco...we had done it once in the ass and he wanted to do it that way too...you bit him...he was pumping gas all day...the only dishes you packed were a bowl, two plates, five glasses and a bottle opener...it didn't seem like you were carrying anything...sitting in the car...putting on make-up.

You said:  Nibble, not bite.

I can barely lift you, let alone throw you...you just started to yell at me to eat something...your eyes did the same thing as they do with me...all my friends told me—Don't move her furniture in there...A wave of jealous heat passed through me.

You say you were drunk or stoned...it was only one night long...you don't have any furniture...you say you like to turn the tables on me...I decided to eat some pretzels.

I went to knock on his door, just to see...you acted like you didn't remember where...that little alarm kept going off in my head...decisions, decisions...you hit my face with your hand...your fist in the air...your teeth on his chest...traffic moving outside.

You said:  He has red hair.
You said:  He's an idiot.

A box of your clothes tumbled down the stairs...I was hungry at first and then you told me...so much yelling and shouting, I can't remember who from (from everyone involved)...you have a habit of calling me Dummy these days.

A guy in a bathrobe answered the door...I couldn't tell what color his hair was...his TV had a pornographic movie showing...I accidentally broke one of the glasses...the straight salty stick kind, not the twist kind...my mouth was jealous and bruised.

Sometimes we would eat breakfast and sometimes I'd leave you naked...when you're nervous it's hard for you to fuck...we used to do it in the car...then he pulled your hair and bit you.

You ordered something greasy—chicken strips or French fries...you had a fork, knife, and spoon...you had a half-bag of sugar...a box of wooden matches and a nut cracker...sometimes a little aggression can help you relax...I took off my glasses and things got blurry.

How are your chicken strips—or French fries?

You laid on your new bed...the guy wore a hat and his robe was loose...I couldn't tell how fat, or old, he was...you don't have a TV but there are magazines in your bathroom...if you were so drunk or stoned why do you remember the biting?

I wanted to eat some of your chicken strips or French fries...I don't like my stomach feeling this way...his hat had the name of a gas station on it...I'm so used to the noise...it really doesn't bother me anymore.

He said:  Forget about it.
He said:  Down the hall.
He said:  Magazines in the bathroom.

A voice in his room says *"You feel so gooood."*...and then the chicken strips...I wish I could throw you further...your underwear spilled out onto the stairs...I called him an idiot.

*creamy bullets*

You had an annoying alarm clock I dreaded waking up to...you took off all your clothes...your back bones stood out...you hugged your knees...he pulled your hair and bit you...you were drunk or eating French fries...something greasy.

If you threw me off a bridge would you trust me more?...a hot wave passed though the room...I told all my friends that we were in love...I mean, I keep seeing your eyes do that thing...like when I talk in your ear...like when you point to your ear and say: Right here.

He says he wants it in the ass...I made a decision to fuck you in the ass...sometimes you bite me...it was like I did all the moving and you just sat there...the rearview mirror...your lipstick...he smelled like gasoline...I recalled my affection for gas fumes as a child...idiot...dummy...I took off all my clothes...I used to want to work at a gas station...all my friends told me I made bad decisions...all my friends eat breakfast with me.

I made a decision to throw your alarm clock out the window...I'll buy you another one...all the traffic outside...do you trust me?

# Fur Coat

So we have a little fucky-fucky. Lenny and I and some bum we pick up from a car crash. The bum says, "You guys are famous and I know you got drugs". Lenny grabs the bum's hand and burns him with a lighter. When we get back to the house the TV is already flickering on channel 89. "Okay bum," says Lenny, "you get your ass up but keep your head down so I don't have to see ya. I'm gonna watch TV while we do it." The bum nods his head toward a pile of cocaine on the coffee table. We give him permission to dull his senses.

I pick up the telephone and start to phone the pay-per-view. "No, no, I like it like this. Just stand behind me and moan like a girl," says Lenny.

"You want me to nibble on your ear?" I ask.

Lenny throws his head back and his ear kinda winks at me or something. My mouth goes all sticky around his fuzzy neck and waxy ears. It reminds me of Butterfinger candy bars. Lenny just watches the TV picture warping and scrambling around the image of a black woman's breasts swinging in circles. Once in a while the sound comes on the speaker and you hear these people on TV say stuff like "oh yeah, fuck me hard, you want my ass, you want to cum in my tight ass." Or other things like that.

"Give me the fuckin' whip," says Lenny. "The whipper, I need more whipper." I grab the old whip cream canister and give it to him with a fresh cartridge twisted on. He takes a long hit, his face turning red and evil. He starts to hit the bum in the back of the head with the canister and the bum flinches madly before collapsing flat on the floor. I twist Lenny back around and grab his prick. He squirts up my arm and we start cracking up, our eyes squished shut as the last drop oozes out. I carefully hold my arm out not to spill a drop and Lenny gets the needle ready. I look at the bleedin' bum on the ground and feel itchy. My left arm tries to restrain itself from my belt and buttonflys. The pump is pulled on the giant-looking hypo and a shitload of Lenny's spunk is filling it up thick and good. He's fuckin' karate choppin his arm and beggin' for a vein to appear. One does, quivering to the surface like an earthquake. He stabs at it and injects the dead sperm back in his system.

"Suck that cock," someone on TV says through the static of the moment. The hypo falls to the ground and Lenny grabs his other needle with God-knows-what in it. He won't give me details. He just says it's his way to have multiple orgasms. "Honey showed me," he said to me once. "She'd fuckin' cum all over my face in splashes when we were into the hard-core shit. She'd take a razor blade to my jizz like it was coke."

I wipe my arm off with a dirty rag and then start wrestling with my pants. Lenny flops on the carpet and holds the groggy bum like a teddy bear. They both sound like they're speaking in tongues, but the bum's inflection sounds more pained. I want a hit off the whipper but there's blood and greasy hair shit all over it. I start on my dick with both hands like I'm playing drums, fast and hard, with a rocket ready to blast off in my stomach. I want to squirt on Lenny's face. When I first met him I wasn't too into that, but he always treats me real sweet for a few days after I do it. "Look at me, Lenny! Fuckin' look at me," I shout. Lenny looks up and I almost lose my climax because I forget he's grown some stupid beard. I've told him before it looks too artsy faggy like the Beatles or some shit. Luckily, when I look away my eyes spot a big poster of Honey on the wall. Damn sexy wife, this poor fuckin' comedian had.

*creamy bullets*

"I want to fuck your wife," I say to Lenny as my surge explodes. "Tangle this shit in her hair," I say as my second shot flies toward my chest. I grab both the hypos off the floor and suck some of my jism into one of them. The beaten bum on the floor twists into a question mark at my feet and his lips creak open into an idiot smile. "Wow," he says, "do you guys have insurance for all this?"

"Later," I say, "We'll talk about it later." My face folds into itself and a sharp biting sensation trickles down my arm and then doubles back through my shoulders and chest. It makes me feel like I'm wearing a fur coat. An imploding fur ball that covers my body with the softness of a lazy dream.

When my eyes feel clean and weightless again, I open them slowly, to be confronted with eager sunlight slapping me in the face. The sound of two men fade in. I look over into the kitchen and see Lenny and the bum wearing new clothes and lighting a circle of candles. Blisters and bruises spot their hands and arms. They're talking about something like it was a secret. The morning newspaper is sprawled on the floor. I can see the front-page story. It's about someone famous being dead.

# The Camp Psychic

My parents put me in a summer camp when I was fourteen because they found some of my poetry and thought I was going to kill a bunch of people. When I say "found" I mean my dad snooped through my notebook. There was a poem about living in the gutters and eating Charleston Chew candy bars and feeling pain and anger in all my being. I didn't really know what a gutter was; I always imagined them to be basement apartments—really narrow ones with just room enough for a small dirty mattress. The Charleston Chew was my favorite candy and I remember thinking I could live off them if I ever had to. Each one was about a foot long and you could freeze them and break them up in little pieces. As far as *pain and anger* go, I think I was just going through a punk phase. It wasn't that I felt really angry about anything, just indifferent. I

⟶ *creamy bullets*

used words like *anger* as default when I didn't feel anything.

My dad was yelling at me in my bedroom, the evidence flopping in his angry right hand. "Are there any drugs in your room?!" he demanded to know. Whenever I did anything he disapproved of, my dad instantly thought I was smoking something. "If I ever see someone selling you drugs, I'll kill them." My dad was small and pale and worked as a pharmacist. He had bad hair like Billy Crystal.

The next day, I heard my mom and dad looking through some pamphlets for summer camps. They were going to send me away. They thought I needed a change of scenery, was becoming too isolated. They wanted me to be part of a group for summer, maybe learn something. They called an outdoorsman camp. It was full. They tried a tennis camp. It had been cancelled. They were told the arts & crafts retreat was good but it was too expensive. I was too old for the Catholic youth getaway. Finally, my mom found one that worked. Being a failed junior high actress herself, she thought it would be good for me to spend the next four weeks at the Walla Walla Drama Camp.

Located in a small wooded area behind a high school, the surroundings looked like the perfect place for amateur child actors pretending to be campers. The tents made me feel like I was in the Army. There were nineteen other kids and five older camp leaders there. One camp leader per tent. The one in my tent was a college freshman named Carlos. My tentmates were Steven, a chubby twelve-year-old whose nose always bled, Todd, a thirteen-year-old rocker who wore leather wristbands and never brushed his teeth, and Dodger, an eleven-year-old Mexican who looked like he was eighteen. He was tall, big, and had a mustache. He even dressed like he was already grown up (tucked-in shirt, dark blue slacks). We got our own cot, two cardboard boxes to keep our stuff in, a flashlight, and some bug spray. Each cot had one crummy pillow that felt like it held a dozen feathers and some left-over cotton candy.

Our first night, we played the usual getting-to-know-you games and passed around a can of sausages before Carlos announced, "There's something you guys need to know about me." I thought he was going to tell us that he committed a crime or something, but instead he said, "I'm gifted in the psychic arts."

No one said a thing at first because we were trying to figure out what this whole psychic arts business was.

"Do you guys know what that means?" he asked finally.

Todd picked at some zits on his neck and Dodger looked down at his white sneakers.

"Does it mean you can tell us our horoscopes?" said Steven.

"Close," said Carlos. "It means I like to eat people." He let his bad joke gain weight with a serious pause and then burst out laughing. "I'm just shitting you," he said. I remember being shocked and delighted by his casual swear and thinking that the camp might actually turn out to be fun. At least I might learn how to swear better.

Carlos grabbed some paper from one of his boxes and passed around some pens. "I want everyone to write down the name of a coin. You know—penny, dime, silver dollar, whatever. In the morning, when I wake up I'll know what you wrote on your paper." We each wrote something down. "Now fold up your paper and put it under your pillow tonight while you sleep." We did as he said. I wrote Nickel.

It took me a long time to fall asleep that first night. I kept shifting in my cot and worrying about what activities we were going to be doing. I had never been in a play and even speaking in class gave me butterflies. Images of Steve Martin with the fake arrow through his head kept swirling in my half-dream thoughts. The images got blurrier and blurrier until they scattered into nothing.

"Rise and shine," Carlos announced the next morning. "It's time to read your little minds."

We rubbed our eyes and sat up. I stuck my hand under my pillow to make sure my answer remained untouched. I had it folded a special way so I could see if Carlos cheated. It hadn't been unfolded. My secret was safe.

Dodger's paper was sticking out of his pillow, about ready to fall on the ground. If Carlos were going to peek at someone's answer, Dodger's would have been easiest. Carlos pointed to the dangling paper and told Dodger to hold it to his forehead. When Dodger held it up I could easily see the answer.

"A half dollar," says Carlos. "Your answer is half dollar."

"I could have told you that," I said. "You can see the answer between his fingers. He didn't even fold his paper."

Carlos waved off my comments. "His mind is just easy to read. Bigger kids have less psychic protection. It's a fact." I thought Dodger was going to tackle Carlos after that comment but he just wadded up his paper and threw it in the far garbage can.

"Okay. I'll do you next," Carlos said to me. I held my paper up to my head. It was folded in a star-shape, a trick I learned from my 6th grade girlfriend, Sheila (we'd gone out for three days before Christmas break ruined it).

With his eyes closed, Carlos took a deep breath. "It's a small one...I see Eisenhower...your coin is a dime."

I unfolded the paper carefully. "Nice try," I said. I held up my paper. It was in all caps: NICKEL.

"Well, no psychic is perfect," he said. He quickly turned to Todd. "Let's me touch your paper." Todd gave him a suspicious look. Carlos reached out and Todd let him pass his hand over the paper. His was folded in a triangle, like the shape we used for playing table football. Carlos snapped his fingers. "Susan B. Anthony dollar," he announced. Todd unfolded his paper. It said silver dollar. "My mind saw S and dollar," Carlos stammered. "I guess my mind can't read your sloppy writing." Todd scoffed and shook his head before folding the paper back into the triangle.

By this time, Steven was visibly shaken by this whole scene. I thought maybe he just had to go to the bathroom but it was his face and hands that mostly spasmed as he held his paper aloft. He'd taken a pencil and blacked out one side of the paper in an effort to conceal his answer. Carlos looked him right in the eye and rubbed his chin intensely. "Steven," he whispered dramatically. "I know you wrote quarter."

Steven took a step back and his mouth started to quiver. "You're right," he said. "I wrote down quarter and then I tried to switch it to penny." He reached under his pillow and pulled out another paper, folded as small and square as a piece of gum. Carlos took it from him and unfolded it quietly and slowly. He held it up. It did, in fact, say in a nervous scrawl, quarter. Steven turned pale and started screaming. Most of the other kids and camp leaders poked their heads into our tent to see what was happening. Carlos tried to calm Steven but he wouldn't stop screaming and pointing his finger at the paper. It was the kind of scream that sounds hollow but full of terror, as if the screamer can't quite get all his breath into his throat. I imagine it's what dolphins would sound like if they screamed. Finally, one of the camp leaders, a ridiculously chesty girl named Nicole, pressed Steven into her green halter top, and led him away to a trailer office. Carlos watched them as they left, his eyes jealous and pained. We never saw Steven again.

I didn't learn a lot during that camp. And I didn't start believing in psychics either. Carlos was just an actor good at playing hokey characters. Dodger never really came out of his shell but he was the best one at playing grown-ups. He was appropriately stiff and creatively dull. Todd was actually pretty impressive. He was still a scrunge, but his acting had more energy than others and he impressed the camp leaders with his range. I was better at exercises where I played supporting parts. I couldn't carry a scene and I couldn't memorize lines. My favorite part of the camp actually was when we played kickball against the fat camp on the other side of the school grounds. We got beat terribly until our last game, when I kicked the winning runs in. I got a merit badge for that.

When my parents picked me up on the last day of camp, Carlos walked over to meet them. He made a big deal about giving me his phone number, like we were going to be friends. But I'm pretty sure he actually hated me. My dad wrote our number down for him in return and smiled like a goon as he shook his hand.

In the backseat of the car, I unfolded the paper and saw that Carlos had written 1-800-JERKOFF. I laughed a little about that but then felt tricked and angry inside. "You gotta be shitting me," I said quietly. My dad turned the radio down and looked back at me with a glare.

"What kind of English is that?" he said.

"I don't know," I answered.

My mom closed her magazine for a second and put her hand on her forehead like she was nursing a headache.

I turned around and looked out the back window, the road blurring past us, each little town disappearing as we sped past. I wished I could read my parents' minds. I wasn't sure what I was worth anymore.

# Flying Horses

I got off my horse and watched the burning body. A fireman approached me with a cup of hot coffee. He gave me a photograph of a naked boy with a large sexual organ. I stuck it in my mouth. He sipped his coffee loudly without looking at me and then excused himself to disconnect a hose. I picked up a five dollar bill that he seemed to have dropped on purpose and stuffed it down my pants. Something seemed to drip from my mouth.

A well-dressed man came up to me and asked about my dark glasses. I rubbed the top of my head and made my hair stick up, imitating the flames. The real flames were being fought by fire fighters. They were coming out of an old lady's mouth. Her teeth popped loudly. I got the feeling the fire fighters weren't trying very hard to stop it.

The man who was talking to me tore off my glasses and ran toward the burning lady. I stood frozen, half-asleep, half in shock. He threw the glasses at the flaming body like someone pitching a ball in cricket. The body looked lifeless, sort of like a statue. The man then picked up the glasses and tried putting them on the woman's face, but he had a hard time getting around the flames. The fireman who gave me the photograph, then tackled the man roughly.

Moments later, a pizza deliveryman arrived on the scene to feed everyone. The fire spread to four or five nearby houses. I found a bench to sit on. A female fire fighter sat next to me and started talking.

"Your Heaven looks just like my Hell," she said.

"What?" I said.

She gave me a sad look, took a bite of pizza, and with her mouth full, began to tell me about Pac-Ten colleges. I watched the burning lady collapse and listened to the female fire fighter. About ten minutes later I noticed we'd somehow gotten closer to the still-burning body. I turned around and discovered the man who had taken my glasses was slowly and quietly pushing our bench closer to the flames.

"You stupid little monkey," the female fire fighter said to him. "Why don't you just go home and adjust the insurance policies like you're supposed to."

The man clenched his fists and fidgeted with his facial expressions, like he was trying to decide if he should hit her or not. I got in between them and offered the man five dollars to go away. He raised it to six and we settled. All of a sudden he looked at ease and even extended his hand to shake. Before getting into his car he stood with the driver door open, laughing repulsively until the fireman threatened to tackle him again.

"You're a one-eyed fool," the female fire fighter said to me.

The rest of the fire fighters were struggling with several powerful hoses while eating pizza at the same time. The water was spraying frantically into houses that weren't even on fire.

I was getting ready to ride my horse back home when I noticed the old lady who had been on fire was standing up and brushing ashes off of her tattered clothes. She seemed to be fine. I almost wanted to help her but felt embarrassed about the cowboy suit I was wearing. She looked nervously at the clumsy fire fighters as she crouched behind a car, and then ran into one of the burning houses without anyone seeing.

I walked over to my horse and untied the rope. I patted her muscular neck and brushed the rough patches of hair on her side. Her silhouette looked awesome in the firelight. I whispered into her ear and let her run home by herself. I felt good despite my blurry vision.

I made my way to the backyard of the burning house that the lady had entered. I found an immaculately mowed lawn next to a large swimming pool and a full-length basketball court. The formerly burning lady was doing lay-ups there. I noticed it was very quiet as I climbed the ladder to the swimming pool high dive. Once on the diving board I noticed she was practicing free throws. Some kind of noise began to emerge from the sky, like a slow helicopter. Beams of light shot across the backyard in every direction. Now, the lady was shooting 30-footers, swishing every time. It was an amazing sight.

After what seemed to be several hours of stunning athleticism, the lady looked up and saw me sitting on the high dive. She made a few last three-pointers before finishing the display with a vicious slam dunk that shattered the glass backboard. Then she threw the basketball precisely into my hands with stunning ease. She walked over to a suitcase by the side of the court and took a clean white piece of paper out of it. She sat at center court and slashed her left wrist several times with paper cuts. When her hand fell off she finally began to bleed and slowly thereafter, she died.

I stood up with the basketball and bounced on the board until I began to feel the tension leave my body. Then I dove. But I can't remember if there was water in the pool or not.

# I Rest Between Them

It started at the merry-go-round. I'm not sure what drew me there. I had no kids and I wasn't a babysitter. I guess it was the novelty of having this big carnival relic inside a fast food restaurant.

I'll go ahead and say it: I was at a Burger King.

Maureen had been running the merry-go-round a long time. It was passed down to her from her father. I didn't ask how it ended up here, at the home of the Whopper. But she charged the company for her services, her machine, and that's how she made her living. It was an attraction. People came from all over the county to see it. There were days when the engine would start to overheat and she'd have to shut it down for a couple hours.

I'd go there on the slower days, sit with Maureen and talk about life. She had been engaged before I met her but she broke it off so she could live with her mom and take care of her. She wore a dress shirt and a tie when she worked the merry-go-round. I figured she was trying to cultivate a formal air, of nostalgia and family fun. She was thin and had a nervous energy like she couldn't wait to get on with something else. She had brown, medium-length hair and eyes that always looked a little stoned. She was fourteen years older than me.

I was on a break from a relationship, meaning I would probably get back into it after I saw how other people felt about me.

Kristi was the girl I was on a break from. We worked at the newspaper together. Not as reporters or anything like that. We worked graveyard shift on the production line, slipping color ad inserts between section B and C before someone else bundled them all up for the vans to deliver to the paperboys. We were one step above the paperboys. Maybe even one step below.

Kristi was the only reason I worked there. I met her on a smoke break three nights in and she kept touching my legs as we sat on the back dock. She started calling me her boyfriend after that and we went out for nine months before she freaked out for good.

"Wanna have lunch with me?" Maureen asked as she started up her ride for a dozen kids.

"Oh, uh, sure. You want a double cheeseburger meal?"

"No. I meant lunch somewhere else. Like O'Connors or something." She gave me a little jab, to seem casual.

I said it sounded like a good idea. We watched the kids going around in front of us, all smiles except for one. There always seemed to be one who wouldn't smile, as if she'd been forced onto the white horse when she wanted the black horse or the ostrich. I kept watching this one unhappy girl hoping she would grin or do something indicating fun. She kept looking at her parents with that look on her face: *Get me off this thing.*


It was strange to see Maureen outside of the Burger King. She looked better in these surroundings. Neon beer lights brightened her cheeks and gave her figure some shadowy angles. Her tie was off and I could see her bra through her shirt. Our conversation seemed to toggle back and forth, her talking about something in the seventies, me talking about something in the eighties. We seemed a little off, our chemistry tethered to poles far away from each other. Still, she ate her onion rings and drank her iced tea as I picked apart some mysterious sandwich. I couldn't remember what it was I had ordered but it was falling apart badly, the bread a little too BBQ soggy, the crispy fried meat (chicken?) too awkward and slick. I got sauce on my cheek and I didn't have a napkin. I used a french fry to squeegee it off. She saw what I was doing and gave me her napkin. I self-consciously put the fry back on my plate. I realized we were eating the same sort of things we would have eaten at Burger King. I felt a sense of futility about this and started to slouch in my seat.

"I think I'm going to take the rest of the day off," she said. "This is fun." I waited for her to elaborate, but she didn't say anything for about three minutes. "I need some new shoes," she finally said. "Let's go to the mall."

I couldn't handle Kristi's mood swings. When we first started going out she'd try to hide them from me. But about four months in, she finally burst. She said it was PMS. All the women in her family had it bad, apparently. Her older sister couldn't keep a job or a boyfriend and her mother had been divorced three times before she even had kids. I said I would try to help her but I wasn't up to the task. I often felt verbally abused and we'd break up almost every month for three days. "We have to talk," she'd say, and my heart would turn to steel. She'd eventually let me know she was better by pinching my butt at work. Or she would walk up to me and simply say, "I suck."

One time at work, we went to my car and made out for twenty minutes. It was about three in the morning; the sky was totally black and draped in humidity. Somehow I was able to bend over enough to put my mouth between her legs. She braced herself against the dash, with her sweats just below her knees, listening for anyone who might walk across the gravel toward us. I tasted her blood and she started to cry. It just made me want her more.

When we went back inside to work I could swear that we stank. But I knew the other people there were not as happy as we were at that moment. They would look out into the sky as it changed color and they wouldn't see what we saw. They wouldn't feel what we felt. Patty Loveless played on the radio and everything was good and comfortable as we slipped the coupons in, just after the box scores and before the obituaries, our eyes looking up and connecting every few moments until the vans pulled up to the docks.

Walking in the mall with Maureen didn't make me feel less self-conscious about being with her. I remembered the days when I actually used to hang out in the mall. Back then, who you walked around with was a sign of your status. If I were seen with one of the popular girls, the other guys would be jealous and maybe give me some respect for a few weeks. But if I was caught shopping with my mom, or some girl from marching band, it was like it went on my permanent shame record.

"I'll make this quick," Maureen said, steering me into a store full of sneakers. She had grabbed my arm for a couple seconds when she said this and it made me think, automatically and uncomfortably, about what it would be like if we were ever a couple. I fell deep and troublingly into this cloudy thought and didn't say a word the whole time we were in the shoe store. It was like I was with a different person all of a sudden. Instead of a person running a merry-go-round, eating French fries, and talking about her favorite Jackie Chan movie, she was just another girl dying for a new pair of shoes. She must have sensed my uneasiness. She settled for a pair of brown suede Converse One Stars. She changed into them once we got out of the store, sitting on a stone bench amid the people passing by. I noticed for the first time that she had nice feet. She flexed her toes and looked at me. "I just wanted some good supportive shoes," she said. "You want me to buy you some shoes?"

"No, it's okay," I said, my voice dry and cracking. She smiled and started to slip the second shoe on.

⟶ *creamy bullets*

"Wait," I said. I touched the heel of her foot and wondered if she was ticklish. Inside my head, I was still thinking too much, internalizing and overanalyzing, but touching her foot, at least for the moment, made me aware of my hand. "Oh," she said. "That feels good." She closed her eyes. I closed my eyes too. "I'm glad we're friends," she said.

Kristi spent every Wednesday morning with her mom, running errands and sometimes drinking Bloody Marys. We had Wednesdays off together and she'd let me sleep until late in the afternoon before she came over and let herself into my apartment.

She woke me up on one of these Wednesdays and put her hand in my boxer shorts, trying to arouse me. I turned over and away from her, not ready to wake up. She exhaled loudly and left the room. I fell back asleep but she kicked open the door ten minutes later.

"I know why you don't want to have sex," she said tightly.

I woke up immediately. I tried to remember what I'd been looking at earlier in the day, when I woke up around noon, when I surfed the Internet, image after image, trying to find just the right one. I never knew when I'd find it but I always did, even if I had to look at dozens of women. It was something I did sometimes several times a week, a few private moments of fantasy. Sometimes, after I'd emptied myself of these urges, that hollow space would fill with shame.

She left my place angry and calling friends on her cell phone. I hated to think what she was saying and what they would say back to her.

She called the next day and we talked more. She was still shook up by the whole thing. "I'm taking some more days off," she told me. She was being very stern. I imagined her standing very stiffly somewhere, close to a highway, her eyes rimmed red, staring at a mountain far away.

Somehow, Maureen and I found ourselves at a jazz club where one of her friends was playing. Some of her other friends were there, too, and I got this weird feeling that they were treating us like we were a couple.

"At first I thought you were her younger brother or something," her friend Scott said to me. His hair was mostly gray with some red. His mouth seemed involuntarily wrinkled into a frown. I swallowed some beer and tried to tell him we were just friends, but he interrupted me. "My first wife was ten years younger than me. Not to say that's a bad thing. I was in heaven for six months." I asked him what happened and he looked at me as if I was getting too personal. "The life experience just isn't there yet. I got tired of being her teacher."

"Are you talking about Mandy again?" Maureen asked him. She grabbed my arm and held on. "Stop telling your horror stories. Are you trying to scare my date away?" I experienced a strange mix of feelings then—I felt defensive about my age and my "life experience," but I was also unexpectedly thrilled that Maureen had called me her date. It was like I had permission to play a role now. I didn't have to be an individual among strangers. I could scoot closer to Maureen and blend into her. I could let her talk and only offer a comment if she asked me herself. It was easier this way. I kept drinking and felt my nerves unwind. The jazz started to sound good as I held hands with Maureen and tried to play footsie under the table.

I told Kristi that I thought I was a sex addict, that I felt the need to ejaculate every day. I told her that I had worried about it for a long time—worried about things like becoming sterile or mentally ill—but the habit had become a part of me. Even if I had sex with her every day, I'd still have to masturbate sometimes. Anything could trigger it. Anyone. It wasn't a matter of her not satisfying me, because she did. The images I looked at weren't competition. But everything I said sounded unfeeling and terrible. Words were dumb.

It's a desire to please myself. To be able to do it whenever I wanted. Without ceremony.

She asked if I'd see someone about it and I said I would. Still, she saw it as a betrayal and couldn't stop imagining me, sitting at my computer, looking at other women. It made every part of her burn.

Maureen came over to my apartment after the jazz band finished that night. My neighbor, a college dropout named Larry, made small talk with us for a little while outside. He was cooking hot dogs for himself on a little barbecue and he kept looking at Maureen like he was trying to remember where he knew her. "Oh wait," he said. "You're the one who runs the merry-go-round at BK." We all laughed and Maureen said quietly that yes, that was her. "I did that too for a while," Larry said. "Down at Oaks Park. I was always nervous that people were falling off." He laughed by himself this time. "It's hard to see around the whole damn thing, you know?"

I told Larry goodnight and he seemed surprised when Maureen and I headed into my place together. I hadn't told him about Kristi yet. "Have a good one," he said.

When Maureen sat on my couch in the front room, I kneeled on the carpet in front of her and held her in an uneven sort of hug. I wasn't sure exactly what

— *creamy bullets*

I wanted. But I did want to feel her body against me. It was so different from Kristi's. She was smaller but not as soft. Even her head seemed different, and smaller. My mouth felt too big for hers. Her hair was short and dry in my hands. Her neck seemed too thin, and dangerous.

The couch was noisy, even though we were moving slowly. We slid to the floor and she took off her shirt. I kissed her arms, her chest, and her back. I found myself staring at her shoulder blades as if I couldn't tell what they were. They stuck out of her skinny frame almost alarmingly, like wings. I rested my face between them.

Outside we heard Larry putting out his barbecue, the water on the charcoals. We could smell the smoke in the air. Maureen tugged my clothes away. She stood up and took off the rest of her clothes. "I have to go home and check on my mom," she said, then she got back down on the floor with me.

The next night I went back to work and my boss called me into his office. He gave me an envelope and told me that Kristi had switched to another dispatch. He said he couldn't tell me where. Inside the envelope was the extra key to my apartment, a bunch of photos, and a note. *Since you like pictures more than the real thing*, it said.

I found my station and started my shift, slipping in the inserts and advertisements. I felt like I was in a trance and wondered if this was a "life experience." When it was time for my break I didn't really want to stop. But the guy taking my spot just stood there waiting. Finally, he tapped me on the back, hard. I went outside and looked around, almost expecting to see Kristi, but also wondering if I could see Maureen in these surroundings. I looked out at the empty parking lot, squinting into the dark, and tried to see the future.

# Headache

Every time I put the big truck into reverse it made that awful sounding BEEP BEEEEP BEEEEP— like an alarm clock that you hit the snooze button on. I woke up knowing that something horrible had just occurred.

My head tapped the steering wheel as I stomped on the brake. I heard the little girl crying, sounding far away. The truck was too loud and so I cut the engine and squeezed my head awake. I was always falling asleep lately and I knew it was getting dangerous.

I always thought the beeping sound would make people move out of the way quickly. But some people do not move quickly. I set the parking brake and climbed out of the cab. She was already dead.

The little girl said—"Grandma?"

I didn't want to make a scene. I got down on the ground and leaned toward the old lady's tight, broken mouth. I could simultaneously feel the final breaths and the stiffening bones of the corpse.

"It's okay," I told the little girl. "She's just asleep."

The girl continued to weep and I looked around to see if anyone noticed. What the Hell were they doing on the site anyway? All sorts of cement mixers, cranes and metal girders everywhere. No place for little girls and old ladies. I saw a bag of groceries under there by her feet. I had a couple dozen 20-foot steel beams on the truck bed and it felt like I'd been maneuvering a jet before I dozed off.

"I'll take care of you," I told the girl. "Your grandma needs to sleep for a while. I think I gave her a headache."

I left the job site without clocking out. The little girl and the stiff old lady were in my Regal Town car and I was driving us to my retarded brother's house. I guessed that the girl was four, five or six years old. The old lady made strange sounds and I told the little girl not to worry, sometimes people speak Russian when they get really bad headaches. I tried to sound calm as I apologized to the corpse for running her over. The girl sorted through the crushed groceries and found a good banana.

*creamy bullets*

At my brother's house, no one was home. There was a baseball game that afternoon and I knew he would be at the stadium selling and throwing peanuts. I opened up a sleeping bag on the floor and zipped the old lady inside. "She just has to take a nap," I told the granddaughter. "Do you want to take a nap too?" I felt a blanket of exhaustion starting to overtake me again.

When I woke up I was lying on the floor next to the old lady and I thought I heard a beeping sound. I instinctively flung my hand toward the sound and pressed down on the stiff lady's breast. The beeping stopped. Some spit bubbles were seen on her lips.

I heard the little girl playing in the bathtub. My brother appeared, entering through the front door with a handful of mail and a baseball bat. The little girl called out: "Are you awake? Hey guys, are you awake!?"

I stood up and put an ignorant look on my face. "Walter—" I started. The little girl skipped out of the bathroom, half wet and half naked. Walter gave me an impatient expression, one he often used when I visited him unannounced. I tried not to stutter as I introduced the body. "This...is..." I shot the girl a Please-help-me look.

"Grandma," she announced.

"Yeah," I said. "It's, uh, Margaret. She has a...uh, she's sleeping."

Walter gave the body a good look-over. The old lady seemed to say something briefly in Russian. Walter leaned down to check her breathing.

"Margaret's not breathing too well," Walter told us. "What's your name?" he asked the little girl.

"Janey," she stated.

Walter lead Janey to the exotic fish room and told her to name all the fish while he made some coffee for his sleepy visitors. Of course, Walter knew the old lady was dead. He was retarded but he wasn't dumb.

I was taking the body out of the sleeping bag when Walter came back into the room. He picked up the baseball bat and delivered three sharp blows to the raggedy body. I tackled Walter to the ground and pried the bat from his hands. "What the Hell do you think you're doing?" I questioned.

Walter shook himself from his violent spell and looked at me shyly. "I just always wanted to beat someone with my bat before. To see what it felt like. I mean she's already dead."

A strange musty smell started to make its presence known. We helped each other off the floor.

Janey came hopping into the room announcing the names of the exotic swimming pets- "Otis is the fat green one. Jojo is the long skinny orange one. The one that looks like a raccoon is Captain Jones. Rodman is the weird-looking black one. The shiny blue one is—Grandma, your headache is better!"

Walter and I spun around to catch sight of the old lady's body suddenly sitting upright and opened eyes looking dazed. She wheezed and coughed and spread her arms in front of her as if to say, *What in God's name happened to my body?*

"Grandma, talk like a Russian again. That was neat."

"I just got back from the promised land," the lady said. "And you there- the touched one," she pointed at Walter and smiled, "You were there, wearing a tuxedo."

Walter looked down at his body, making sure he wasn't dead or wearing a tux.

"Janey dear, come help me up honey."

The little girl went and held the old lady's hand.

"Oh my," said the grandmother, "I do believe my legs are crushed."

Right at that moment I began to think of ways to get the lady to the hospital anonymously. My head started to hurt and a loud beeping sound filled my ears. I felt a heavy pain going through my own legs. I reached down and my hands were quickly smashed. My vision cleared and I found myself underneath a large truck of some kind. I knew something horrible had happened. There were vegetables, a gallon of milk, toothpaste, and a bag of Doritos in disarray where my body splayed on the gravely ground.

I heard footsteps coming toward me. My throat choked out dark blood and dry, clumsy chunks of language. There was a little girl's voice calling my name. A headache filled my body.

# Outside of This Place

Last week, I noticed my hair was falling out in unusual fashion. As in the location of my body of the falling out. As in my arm pits and crotch.

I began to suspect our upstairs neighbor. We saw her once washing the concrete steps with chicken blood. Some kind of voodoo routine.

This lady got unpleasantly pissed off at my wife and I when we first moved in and couldn't produce a corkscrew for her. She seemed agitated while watching me annihilate the wine cork with a Philip's screwdriver.

My wife has not noticed a change in the health of her hair. She shaves her whole body anyway. Except her head of course.

Another tenant recently told us that she has seen the inside of Voodoo Lady's apartment. There was construction paper laid out everywhere with all sorts of chicken parts spread out on top. At least it looked like chicken. There was a bucket of blood on the dining room table, placed neatly between the salt and pepper shakers. This tenant told us she only saw the place that once, while borrowing the telephone.

I am in bed, crawling over my wife, trying to locate her left nipple in the dark. Her right foot is gently massaging my groin. I become large. She says in a concerned voice: "Fuzzy."

I nearly lose my concentration but keep on licking. Her body so hard and smooth.

"Stubble," she says, under her breath. My body starts to numb and I look at the glowing numbers of the clock: 4:12 AM.

"I need a drink," she tells me as her fingers click on the bedside lamp. Standing beside the bed, she pauses. Her body is spotted with three dark hairs in the shapes of an S, a 6, and a C. She lightly brushes them off. She looks a little concerned.

She exits the bedroom and I stare at the bed and the floor beside it, the troublesome nests of hairs.

My wife comes back in with a glass of Kool-aid that we share. Upstairs, we hear the lady turn her vacuum cleaner on.

I go upstairs the next afternoon and offer her a ribbon-wrapped corkscrew. She opens the door with some kind of strange robe on. The bottom half is some kind of red velvet, but above the waist is more like a see-through pink chiffon. Her large brown breasts rest just above her deep belly button, which looks about the size of a bathtub drain.

I look at her nose when I talk to her. "I got you a present so you don't have to use my Philip's screwdriver again."

"And where's the wine, sweet man?" She tests the sharp point of the corkscrew with her index finger.

"Sorry," I lie to her. "I have to go to work."

"I thought you worked at nights," she says.

I wonder how she might know when I work. I hardly spoke to her until now.

"I can hear you working come night time down there."

I start to understand what she's getting at, and she smiles like a psychic.


After she burrows around in a kitchen cabinet for a few minutes, she brings out a bottle of dark red wine.

I sit in an overstuffed chair in the living room and watch a soap opera I have never heard of.

"I think this will be adequate for starters," she says, rubbing the bottle against her chest. By this time, I have surveyed the area and find nothing too unusual about her place. There are some lurid Aztec-looking pictures on the wall and a crowded bookshelf with all sorts of religious books. Everything from Buddhism to Mormonism. Her vacuum cleaner is leaning in the corner but the carpet still looks dirty. We drink and she tells me her name is Brenda.

She sits on the couch and opens a photo album in her lap. "Come look at this picture over here," she tells me. I sit beside her and see a photograph of her standing in front of a familiar building.

"That's what the outside of this place looked like ten years ago," she says. "It's a nicer shade of blue and the shrubs look a good dose livelier." She puts the heavy album on my legs and then straightens her posture, holding her breasts up for a second. "It's funny how ten years can wear shit down."

In the photo, Brenda looks almost like a teen-ager; 20 pounds lighter, skin darker, her back straight as a board. On the opposite page there is a photo, taken more recently it looks like, of her holding a snake.

"How old are you?" I ask.

"I'll be 40 next year," is her answer. "Look some more if you want."

I turn a few pages, seeing photos of her at beaches, at parties, at formal gatherings, with relatives. There was one that showed a white guy with a big mustache kissing her neck from behind and pushing up on her breasts with his hands. It embarrasses me for some reason, arouses me maybe.

An hour later, a tall young girl comes out of one of the bedrooms. She looks part Hispanic and has a word or something tattooed on the side of her neck. She makes a deep sound in her gut as she sits down in the chair I sat in earlier.

"What kind of shit-juice is that?" she asks right off the bat, indicating my wine glass.

"Some kind of red wine," I say, trying to sound friendly but tough.

She stares at it with a grimace, looks in the kitchen at Brenda, who is looking for more wine, then looks at my shoes. "I don't drink," she says. "I got a job."

I start to lean forward for my glass, but catch myself and pretend to wipe dust off the table instead. "Where do you work?"

"Safeway," she says, in a tone of voice suggesting I should already know. "I take groceries out to your car."

"Doesn't it get boring?"

"I do lots of shit there. It's cool. We play the radio loud at nights when we're stockin' the shelves."

It makes me feel intrusive, but I ask her anyway: "Do you live here?" I drink the last drops of my wine and Brenda comes up behind me with another bottle.

"I'm just staying for a little longer," she says. "M makes me feel safe."

"M?"

"That's what she calls me," Brenda explains.

"What do you mean by safe?"

The girl looks at the clock and yawns before answering. "A couple of weeks ago this big fat guy raped me in the back of a van after I took his groceries out. He was a guy I remember because he tried to pick up on one of my friends the week before at a party. I didn't want to go to the police, so I came to M. She can fix guys without even touching them."

I don't know what to say. Sometimes I get the feeling that sympathy is useless. I start to feel uncomfortable and wonder if my wife is home from work yet, if she is wondering where I am.

"I want romance," the girl says, somewhat out of the blue. "Guys don't seem to understand the general idea of being decent. I think they can be decent without waving a gun around, don't you?"

*creamy bullets*

"Nice guys don't feel exciting to some women," I concede. "We have to capture your attention with bravado and physical violence."

Brenda pours more wine in my glass and hers, then shakes her head. "That's why magic is on our side. That's why feminine power is everywhere. Maybe invisible to some, but everywhere—like some think God is."

"Men are forgettable; they don't linger," says the young girl. I notice that her tattoo says: *Hybrid* or maybe *Heartbreak*. The letters are written in a leaning, Victorian-style cursive.

Brenda intervenes on the subject: "I'd like to see what men would do if the tables were turned, if we were in the position of physical power and they had to walk scared at night."

My head starts to feel light and I rub my scalp instinctively; it seems to shuffle around like a wig. I subtly scan the room for a phone, but don't see one. I hear the sound of a shower turning on. The young girl is gone from the room in what seems to be a split moment, stretched out like taffy. I notice Brenda by the door, fastening the latch, and then locking the door.

"She still doesn't feel clean," Brenda says as she walks toward me. "I hope the shower doesn't bother you downstairs." Her hand squeezes my shoulder and then relaxes. Her fingers fall down my arms like water. "Does it bother you?" she says in more of a whisper.

My throat feels scratchy and paralyzed. I look at her and want to say, "Fix me. Fix me."

large

# Reunion

He wondered who they all were, this family of his. There were three clans here, clustered around several picnic tables at the largest State Park in Oregon, and he could barely distinguish his own. David was a Sullivan. Then there were the Cardells and the Wellers.

Families confused him, mostly because he never gave them any thought. Shouldn't they all be Sullivans? Why are his aunt and uncle named Weller? Why are the Cardells mostly half-Mexican or half-black?

His mother, a small bear of a woman named Dora, tried to explain it to him before. But he was a young brat and refused to focus on the path of her words, their genealogy. He daydreamed until nothing real stuck to his brain. It would be uncomfortable to ask her now. He was 38, still working the kind of jobs that seemed cool fifteen years ago, but sad now—record store clerk, dance club doorman, stadium vendor/peanut thrower. Currently, he worked as a ticket taker at a discount movie theater. Just over nine dollars an hour, but he got free popcorn and soda. He had to wear a nametag. It said, *David...Director.*

David wondered if anyone else at the family reunion made less money than he did. He had learned you can't gauge how much someone makes by how they look. Some of his cousins, even a few nephews, looked poor as hell but made three times as much as he did, working construction or landscaping. Most of the Sullivan/Cardell/Weller family plodded their way through life with whatever rewards a GI Bill or GED could get them. College was a foreign concept to their teens, scads of pimply youths that viewed higher education with anxiety and suspicion. He counted ten of these kids among the fifty or so adults present. There were some younger ones as well. Two babies, a toddler with dirt or food caked around its mouth, and a pair of ten year olds who hovered around the picnic table of sweets, punching each other and sometimes swearing. One of the longhaired biker types of the family, presumably a father, urged them to "eat something healthy." He gave them each a carrot. They used them as swords before tossing them into a bed of burnt charcoal.

Shading the sun from her eyes, Francine, David's new girlfriend, grew restless in her lawn chair. David rubbed her shoulders from behind and wished he could remember more names. Some of them he hadn't seen in twenty years. A tall black man approached David and Francine. His t-shirt said *King of Beers* and he wore his kinky hair in a style that looked similar to a mullet. He held out a large hand. "Uncle David," he said. "It's been a long time."

David squinted and groped in his memory for a name. "Roger?"

"Ricky," the man corrected him.

"Oh my God," said David. "I used to give you basketball lessons. Now you're a foot taller than me. What happened?" His clichéd conversation skills embarrassed him sometimes.

Ricky rubbed his chin with one of his hands and smiled. "Once I got into high school, I just started growing."

David introduced him to Francine and then took the opportunity to get the lowdown on some of the others at the reunion. "Those are my two kids," Ricky said, pointing out two huge teens that looked like offensive lineman. "And you probably saw my mom, and there's Randy and Gary and Jeff." As his nephew pointed people out, David trapped each face in his sight, aging them backward like computer animation until he remembered them. David himself was young-looking and was convinced that he hadn't changed much besides the glasses he started wearing after turning thirty. "Here comes your family," Ricky said, nodding his head in the direction behind David.

David turned around and saw them, his brother Paul, his mother Dora, and his father, James. Paul lugged a large ice cooler awkwardly in front of him, banging his knees and shuffling his sore hands on the handles. He was probably the most successful of the family. At least the most recognized. He was a sports announcer for a local television station and he looked the part—broad shoulders, square jaw, easy-going eyes, coiffed hair. Paul was two years older than David. They were close growing up, playing football with the neighborhood kids, making up comedy routines, throwing snowballs at cars in the winter. Their father was a small but fiery man who commandeered their childhood home with an unpredictable temper and a Catholic style of parenting that stopped shy of compassion. His rule, when it came to what he saw as his children's bewildering behavior, was often denouncement before understanding. Once, when David and Paul were playing an imaginary ghost game in their backyard with some other neighborhood kids, their father came out yelling something about sacrilege and then spanked them in front of the other kids. Word got around the elementary school the next day and none of their friends would come over to their house after that. Talking to their father was impossible and it was never easy confiding in their mother.

When Dora and James started to sleep in separate beds, and later, separate rooms, it made the silence of the home even louder. David and Paul reasoned at some point, probably during their early teen years, that it was because Dora and James were older than most of their friends' parents. Dora was forty-three when David was born. He was an accident. Maybe Paul was too.

"A little help?" Paul said to David, nodding at the cooler. David jogged over. He grabbed one of the handles and they made a space on one of the tables for it. "I'm not as strong as I used to be," Paul joked in an old man voice. He stuck his hand out to his younger brother for a shake. They were not the hugging kind of family. Their father would not allow it. "You keep staying away for longer," said Paul. He searched his mind for a calendar but gave up when he noticed Francine. David introduced them.

"I've heard a lot about you," Francine said. She was already starting to feel a little boxed in, like she had to be the polite girlfriend with a smile on her face. She wasn't part of the family and wasn't sure if she'd ever be. Everything she did felt like it was from a script she didn't have a chance to read before the reunion.

A crackle of feedback sounded behind Paul and David. It was their father. David turned and saw how he had deteriorated since he last saw him. He was in a motorized wheelchair now, the result of a stroke the year before. Although his body was always small, it now looked slack and lifeless instead of sturdy and strong. His spotted right hand rested, twitching next to a controller that powered his chair. A pilled wool blanket wrapped around his waist and legs. He wore a blue flannel shirt that looked too big for him and a brown newsboy hat. Because he could barely speak above a whisper, Dora had recently bought a headset microphone that he struggled to use. An amplifier, the size of a first aid kit, hung squealing from the side of his chair. His left hand swatted helplessly at the volume knob. "Hello, David," he was finally able to say. It sounded like someone dying of thirst, alone in the desert, throat full of sand, walkie-talkie to his dry lips.

"Hi, dad," David said. He took his father's hand and shook it. It felt like picking up an empty glove.

"Are you…going…to stay…weekend?" It seemed to take him forever to say these few words.

"We have to leave on Sunday." David looked at Francine. Talking to his father was already excruciating.

"I'm...James," David's father said to Francine. He tried to smile but even that was a challenge.

"Hello, Mr. Sullivan. I'm glad you were able to come out." Francine felt sad for saying such a thing.

"James," David's father said again. "I'm...James."

"We'd better help with the food," said David. He gently pressed Francine to where his mom stood.

"I'll get the football," Paul called over to him. "Let's show some of these kids how to play." He ran back to his car.

David could sense that Paul wanted to get away from their father too. He remembered one time when their mom and dad got into a fight that Paul tried to break up. Their father slapped Paul over and over, daring him to slap back. "This is my house and nobody attacks me in my house," their father said. "This house needs order." David hid in his bedroom when these fights happened. He put his hands over his ears and cried. Later, Paul told David that the fight was about another woman. Their mother said he was having an affair with someone from church. David wasn't really sure what an "affair" was. But that summer before junior high school he learned the definition of that word and one other: *will*. Paul surprised David one night when he asked him to write out a will with him. David thought it was just a game until they signed each other's will.

"Well, hello there, David," his mom said, walking over to them. "This must be Francine." They stood there, in the middle of all the picnic tables, talking for several minutes. David found himself relieved to be talking with a relative he actually knew and it seemed like Francine was finally comfortable. Just a few feet behind them, he noticed his father nodding to sleep in his chair. Every once in a while, even when he wasn't trying to speak, a yelp of feedback came out of his amp.

"Is this thing on?" Paul said, pretending to tap on a testy microphone. He had snuck up behind David with the football. "It's just like in the movies," he said. "I have an announcement to make." He made a high-pitched feedback sound in his throat and laughed. They walked over to the area where the grass was greener and softer and began tossing the ball. David saw Francine watching them from the drink table.

"Did you hear about Bo?" Paul asked him. Bo was a Cardell. A Mexican with a wife fifteen years younger than him named Janey. Distant hairy cousins.

"I heard Janey left him for a P.E. teacher," David said.

"Then Bo tried to commit suicide by jumping off the roof of their house. On a pile of bricks and glass."

"Shit. Is he okay?"

"No, but he's not dead."

Roger and some of his family came over to start a game. A couple of the young boys were just friends of Roger's kids. David wondered why they would come to someone else's family reunion. One of them had a girlfriend standing away from everyone else. She was sunning herself in a small red bikini that barely held her. David couldn't help looking as she rubbed lotion across her chest and belly. She had dyed blonde hair and the body of a personal trainer. Even though she was wearing sunglasses, David could tell that she had caught him gaping at her.

Paul organized everyone into teams. Five on five. Since he was the sportscaster, they listened to his organizing and rule making. They had about thirty yards to play on. The endzones were marked by a barbecue pit and an inexplicable patch of dead, brown grass, where it looked like a UFO had landed. David was on Paul's team. He lined up in wide receiver position with Paul playing quarterback. There were no huddles, but Paul yelled a play over to David before each down. Deep post, hitch, quick slant. Plays they perfected when they were younger, quicker, and more in shape. They played for twenty minutes before David started to feel his right foot cramp. He quit playing after diving for a catch that skimmed off his fingertips. He walked lightly over to Francine, trying to hide his pain. She seemed distant and cold to him. She got up to help his mom set out more food.

"You work in movie place for movies?" someone called to David. It was another cousin or nephew. David wasn't sure. This one was Korean and very short. "Movie guy," he said to David. He struggled with his English.

David was trying to figure out who this man was. He figured he was probably about twenty years old, though barely five feet tall. "I'm David," he said in a loud voice. He noticed some of the other relatives watching them with pained concentration. "I work at a movie theater," he said a little more quietly. Was he a Weller? he wondered. No one stepped in to help.

The man said his first name and held his hand out. David wasn't sure if he heard him correctly. "Phat?" he said. The short man was doing that thing where a normal handshake turns into a series of complicated positions and gestures, before frowning and letting go suddenly.

"David," his mom shouted over. "Take your father for a walk."

"Okay," he said back to her, though he wasn't sure what she meant. He walked over to where his mom and Francine were cutting sandwiches into tiny squares. His father was just behind them, his wheelchair possibly stuck in the grass.

"He's getting bored," his mother said. "Just go push him around the park or something for a while."

David looked at Francine, who gave him a serious look. He didn't like being around her when she had that look. Maybe she was just bored too. He felt like he was disappointing her somehow. He looked over at Paul and saw him still playing football with the others. After each play, his brother would lift his shirt and wipe the sweat from his face. "Okay," said David. "I'll be back."

He pushed his father through the grass a little until they got to a narrow path. It looked to be paved with black tar and made the heat feel more intense. He never liked to be alone with his dad. Before the stroke, his father would start every conversation with, "Are you still going to church?" But that would take him too long to get out now. Every word was an immense strain for his father. David enjoyed the silence.

"Baff-room," his father then said. He pointed a frail hand at a gray brick building. David pushed him in that direction. He noticed then that he could hear his father's breathing through the little speaker, brittle and hoarse. They tried the door to the men's room but it was locked. David knocked to see if someone was using it and a string of grunts answered his query. His father looked wearily to the women's door. "I don't care," he whispered.

David tapped on the door before pulling it open. "Girls?" he called awkwardly into the empty space. He pushed his father in and opened one of the stalls. "Stand or sit?" David asked him. His father was already unzipping his pants and trying to stand. David locked the wheels on the chair and gingerly grabbed under his arms and tried to pull him up. He found it more difficult than he expected. Dead weight, he thought to himself. His father braced against the toilet paper holder and David moved behind him into an easier position. He heard his father urinate in the toilet. He thought about the times his father shamed him for wetting his bed as a child. "You're not a young man until you stop that nonsense," his father had told him. "I guess you're a baby until then," he would say with a smirk. He heard his father sigh and slowly zip back up. David helped him back into the chair. He wished someone were there to help. His father looked pitiful and slack the way he sat in the chair now. He crouched in front of the wheelchair and tried pushing him into a better posture. The girl in the red bikini came in and saw them this way.

"Oops," she said, and backed away.

"Wait," said David, but she was already gone. He unlocked the wheels and pushed his father back outside. He saw the girl dart into the men's room and heard the door lock. He grabbed the door handle but didn't pull. It felt warm.

He went back into the women's room and washed his hands. "Sorry," he said to the wall, wondering if the girl could hear him.

He came out and saw his father scooting back in the direction of the picnic area. "Hey," he shouted, and was surprised at how angry he sounded. He jogged to his father and stopped him. "I want to keep going," he said. He turned the chair around and watched his father's hand drop helplessly away from the motor control. The sound of the crackling speaker mixed with the sound of the hot wind through the trees. It sounded like a small fire. David reached over and found the volume knob. He turned it up until the speaker squealed. He thought his father said a word underneath it all. "Don't" or maybe "Damn it." David laughed a little before turning it down. He looked back at where the reunion was and saw that nobody was watching them. He pushed the chair in the direction of the water. There was an empty dock a little ways down, swaying like a mirage.

"I have some things to say," David started. He was glad he didn't have to look at his father's face as he spoke. "When I turned sixteen, I decided I wanted to kill you, or something like that." He caught himself backing away from his words as soon as he said them. His father didn't respond though, so his confidence came back, like a tide crashing into sharp rocks. "I wanted to poison you at first but I didn't know how. One time I put firework powder in your soup but you just got sick and went to bed early. Do you remember that?"

The speaker filled with heavy breathing but no words.

"The next morning I was in the kitchen and I thought you were dead because you usually got up earlier than I did. I sat there and I ate about five bowls of cereal in a row. I thought if I could finish the whole box of cereal and you still hadn't made it out of bed, then you were probably dead. But then you came in right before I finished and I just started crying and ran to the bathroom and threw up all the cereal. The bathroom really stank because you threw up in there too that morning. You just yelled at me and made me clean it all up."

David stopped a moment, wiped some sweat from his forehead. He took a napkin from his pocket and dabbed his father's forehead too. He looked over at the bathrooms and saw the bikini girl, watching them and talking on her cell phone. "It's getting fucking hot," David said. It was the first time he swore in front of his father. He started pushing again.

"Didn't you ever know you were a shitty dad?" David asked. "I want you to answer that question." His father started to say something but was stuck, dry-mouthed, on some hard consonant. "It's a yes or no answer," said the son. "Well, I thought you knew the answer. You always had the answers back then. You were never wrong."

They were getting far away from the reunion. He looked back and saw Paul running in their direction. He pushed the wheelchair faster.

"About a month after that, I was going to suffocate you in your sleep. I walked in your room one night with a pillow. I even had duct tape so I could tie you down first but I started to worry about someone finding the duct tape with your hair on it or something. I was going to ask Paul to help but I never did." He looked back and saw Paul talking to the girl by the bathroom. "Paul did pretty good for himself," David said. He stopped and turned the wheelchair 180 so his father could see Paul and the girl, just far enough away so they looked like small blurry shapes. "Paul did pretty good for himself," David said again. "I never really knew what I wanted to do. I felt stuck because I was preoccupied with killing you." David turned his father's chair back toward the dock and started toward it again. They were silent for what felt like a long time. "I didn't know I was going to do this," David finally said, and more long silence followed.

By the time they got to the dock, David's mouth felt dry and his father seemed to be dozing off in the heat. David knelt down on the end of the hard wooden dock and reached a hand into the cool water. He splashed his face and let some of the water get into his mouth. He swished and spit back into the river. "So I killed someone else," said David. "I thought that would help me over the hump, you know. Like, I could just imagine that it was you or something. But it didn't really work that way. I still feel stuck. That was ten years ago." He walked over to his father's wheelchair and pushed it to the end of the dock. He was lying about the murder but he wanted his father to be scared of him, to feel fear in that same sick way he felt as a kid. "If I stand behind you here, do you see what that feels like? You don't have far to go. You're stuck now too."

His father's hands started to shake wildly and the volume was turned up on the little speaker. "Sorry," the voice said. It screamed on top of the feedback like an awful bird. "Sorry," it repeated.

David backed away and started crying. His eyes were blinded by tears and sweat and he couldn't see. The sound of his father's wheelchair crunching over the wood made him cry harder. "I'm sorry, too," he answered quietly. He wiped at his face in a panic and started hyperventilating. He couldn't hear anything except his own grief. When his eyes were finally able to dry, he saw his father steering his wheelchair back off the dock and onto the trail.

David sat there on the dock, wondering if he should go after him. The sun moved behind a cloud and the pounding heat let up for a moment. David thought he heard a splash behind him but saw nothing when he turned around. He looked into the water, concentrated on it. After he jumped in, he struggled to paddle in place. He scanned the water for any living thing. Something to save him.

# Songs for Water Buffalos

S hane received word the week before that Raul had died.

"How did Raul die?" I asked.

"The letter said he died from swelling of the body," Shane said. He picked his nose a little as he said this. He seemed mostly puzzled about it.

Shane and I worked the evening shift at the music store. I'd only known him for a month but already I found him noble for being a sponsor of a starving kid in Bolivia. He wasn't married and he didn't have children of his own, so maybe it wasn't hard for him to do. He wanted to make himself more useful now that he was thirty, he told me before. Twenty-five dollars a month is what he'd been sending.

"It's weird," I said, "you and I couldn't live off twenty-five bucks a month."

"That's because we're American," he said with a bit of antagonism.

I asked how long he had been sending money.

"Only about six months," he said.

I wanted to say something about how odd it was that his kid died even though he had a sponsor. I wondered if an extra five bucks a month would have helped. I also wondered if maybe Raul's real parents or grandparents or whoever got Shane's money spent it on other things instead of food and medicine. Maybe it was spent on cigarettes or beer. I kept quiet and didn't say any of this. That would have been thinking out loud and it wouldn't have been considerate of Shane's current mood.

"I got a thank you letter from him just a month ago," he said. "He did a drawing for me too. There was a bunch of brown kids and a white guy standing in the middle. I guess I must've been the white guy."

Libby was working too. She was standing over by the listening stations, restocking CDs. There was some crazy rock-rap remix playing through the store's sound system but she could still hear some of what we were talking about. She was young and idealistic. Her tight pink dreadlocks sprang wildly around her face as she bobbed her head to the beat. Whenever she smiled, her freckles lit up like stars against the smooth cocoa of her face.

"I have a good idea," she said. "We can raise 250 dollars and buy a water buffalo."

I watched her face to see if she'd explain but she seemed to think we knew the value of a water buffalo. Instead of saying Great idea! or Okay! I said, "Why?"

"A needy third-world family can benefit greatly from having a water buffalo," she said. It was like she worked for some kind of Water Buffalo Company or something. I thought she might pull out a pamphlet at any second. Shane actually turned the music down a little to make sure he was hearing her.

"They can produce milk for a family to drink or sell and they're good for pulling farm equipment and eventually having calves too," she said.

"What do you mean by calves?" Shane asked.

"Baby buffalo," she explained. "Sometimes another family will have a buffalo of the opposite sex and they can breed with them and share or sell the calves. If we get ten people to donate $25, we can really make a difference," she said.

I almost laughed when she said we could make a difference. It just seemed like a weird concept. She was always saying shit like that though.

Shane pulled out his wallet and I, swayed suddenly by the mood of good will, started writing a game plan.

A week later, we'd racked up $150. Libby had printed up a big color photo of a water buffalo and propped it up by a makeshift donation jar by the registers. I got the feeling people thought it was a joke. They probably thought we split it up at the end of each day. Our manager, a guy named Rod who wore those tinted prescription glasses and silk shirts, didn't seem to mind. Or at least he wasn't going to say anything to Libby, who he often thought about as he masturbated in his office.

"Nice buffalo display," he told her. He stared at it for a long time, in deep thought. Shane and I watched him with interest. We thought he might finally donate. "Is there any way we can utilize this to promote a CD?"

Shane and I cringed a little.

"What's that?" asked Libby.

Shane and I tensed up more, fearing an anti-capitalism tirade about to happen.

"Maybe if people bought the new U2 album we could donate a couple dollars to the bucket," said Rod. It was evident that he was trying to sound like he'd thought about it long and hard. "They have a song about a water buffalo, don't they?"

"What are you talking about?" grimaced Libby. "We're not doing this to sell units." She said *units* like it was the root of all evil. "The best thing you can do to help with this, is give some money," she told him.

Rod got a little defensive. "These *units*, Libby, are what make your paycheck possible. And if you asked me more nicely, I probably would donate something."

I can't remember what we had playing on the sound system while this was happening, but whatever it was ended and the store didn't so much as fill with flat silence, as suffocate in it.

Shane and I went out that night and drank some beer at the Black Bear. It was the kind of place filled with picnic tables and benches instead of regular tables and chairs. They had a hundred beers on tap and a clientele consisting mostly of bike messengers. I'd been a regular customer for ten years, ever since I got a fake ID at eighteen. When I turned 21 I started using my real ID and the bartenders just laughed about being duped for so long.

Shane had invited Libby to join us but she was going to some sort of women's book club meeting. She'd been plowing through a 500-page Margaret Atwood novel all day at work.

"Maybe we should organize a benefit or something," Shane suggested. He was one beer ahead of me.

"Who would we get to play for a water buffalo?" I said.

"Are you kidding me? We could get all sorts of bands. Just have Libby ask them. Who can say no to Libby?"

"What do you think about Libby, anyway?"

Shane finished off his third porter and looked around before answering. "She's cool. But she can be kind of preachy too, I guess. Like when she bosses people around at work."

"No, I mean, do you think she's cute?"

Shane scooted his empty glass to the edge of the table and shrugged. He took his time to think of an answer though he already knew it. It was something he thought about a lot. "Yeah, I guess," he said. "I'm not a big fan of the dreadlocks though. I like the pink, just not the clumps."

"I heard that stuff is made out of fertilizer."

"What, dreadlocks?"

"Yeah, like some kind of poop."

Shane thought about this for a second. He looked around and nodded toward a forty-ish guy with dreadlocks wearing a Clash T-shirt. "You should go ask that guy over there," he told me.

"No way, man."

"I'll buy you a beer if you do."

I got up without saying a word and walked over by the guy. He was hanging out with two girls that I'd seen in the record store before—Gwen Stefani wannabes. I leaned over and asked them if I could borrow their salt. I walked back to Shane.

"You didn't ask him," he said.

"I didn't have to ask. I smelled."

"Nice," he said. "Nice and covert. Was it poopy?"

"Like a day-old diaper," I said.

Libby walked in just then. She spotted us, gave us the thumbs up, and went to the bar to order a beer.

"Why don't you just take a good whiff of her hair when she gets over here," I said to Shane.

"Shut up," he said. "No more poop talk."

She walked over with a pint of local beer, lemon wedged on its lip.

"How was the poop talk?" I asked. "I mean, book talk."

"There were only three people there this time. And no one even read the whole book." She squeezed a little lemon onto her tongue. "You'd think that literacy was dead or something."

"It is," I said. "Anyone that reads books is a rebel."

"You don't read books," Shane scoffed.

"I'm not a rebel," I said.

Shane got up to get more beer for himself. "Want another one?"

I shook my head as Shane started his squeeze to the bar.

"We were just talking about the water buffalo," I said to Libby. "Shane wants to help set up a benefit. You know some band guys, don't you?"

She listed off eight band names in a row, only a couple of which I've heard of. I nodded and raised my eyebrows like I was impressed. I could see Shane coming back with his beer, slowing behind her, crouching down with his nose out. I wondered what she smelled like too.

The Ugly Mug Café was kind enough to let us do the fundraiser in their space. It was a large room, big enough to hold a hundred people. It was nearly full.

A band called Hand Over Fist was playing first. Shane and I were working the door (five bucks a head) and Libby had a table in the corner that neatly displayed information and photographs of water buffalo. She also made buttons and T-shirts with water buffalo on them just for the occasion. People seemed more interested in the oddly fashionable image of the buffalo as opposed to its actual humanitarian benefits.

Rod came up to Libby's table and enthusiastically launched into a business idea that would, he

*creamy bullets*

said, "pay for a hundred buffalo." Libby listened considerately as Rod laid out his ideas for water buffalo bags, bumper stickers, coffee mugs, baseball caps, designer jackets, lunch boxes, action figures, mouse pads, pillows and so on. "To go along with the buttons and T-shirts," he said. "You could donate thirty percent to the water buffalo foundation or whatever they're called."

Libby's patient smile turned to a grimace. "Thirty percent?"

Up on the small stage, Hand Over Fist's grinding emocore was plodding to an end. The singer rolled himself into a fetal ball behind the tall bass player, howling the last of his vocal cords away.

Shane nodded in Rod's direction. "How many restraining orders do you think he has?"

"I heard he got one from Liz Phair."

"Really?"

We took money from more people as the second band set up. They were called American Heritage. They had CDs with artwork lifted directly from the cover of the American Heritage Dictionary, fourth edition. They had a good following and played a weird kind of Bruce Springsteen meets Radiohead alt-rock. Out of the four guys in the band, two of them had either gone out with Libby or they were her cousins. I wasn't really clear on which.

Libby came over and worked the door with Shane as one of her friends took over the water buffalo table. I went outside to get stoned with the drummer of Hand Over Fist. I'd seen him in our store a few times but didn't really know him. "These guys suck," he said about American Heritage as we exited.

"Good set," I said. "The people of Tanzania thank you."

"The what?" said the drummer. He impatiently tried a number of keys on the back door of the band's van before finding the right one. We climbed into the back and scooted cases and gear to make room for our smokeout. He pulled a classy J-shaped pipe out of a toolbox and started packing it. It looked to be carved from wood. The sort of pipe that Sherlock Holmes would toke from. The drummer inhaled the first hit and passed it to me with great care, his face reddening.

"I shouldn't be gone long," I said. The pipe felt good in my hands though, like a saxophone. I felt like Charlie Parker.

I walked back in during American Heritage's last song. I didn't realize I was gone for nearly an hour. Rod was working the door by himself as Libby and Shane hopped excitedly near the front of the stage. "We got ourselves two buffalos," Rod told me. He held up a Swisher Sweets Cigar box with money sticking out on all sides. I gave him the thumbs up and smiled with eyes half-closed. He could probably tell I was baked. Libby ran over and gave me a hug when the song was over. She said something to me but I was distracted by her dreadlocks bouncing on my cheeks. I swallowed her scent and imagined my body melting into hers for five beautiful seconds.

As we loosened, I was blindsided by someone wearing a horned Viking helmet. It was Rod, celebrating the night's success too enthusiastically. The manager of the café, a former prison guard named Hector, thought we were fighting. He came over and pulled Rod off of me and told me I had to leave. "No, no, no. He's cool," said Rod, offering to help me up. Hector crossed his arms and served us a cold hard frown. Libby walked back to the stage and started talking to the American Heritage guys as they sold CDs to a couple fans. The last band, The Vikings, were setting up. They were the kind of group that dressed up in Nordic war attire and clomped through a short set of songs that they turned into epic improv freak-outs. Shane came over to me and asked if I saw American Heritage.

"I had a meeting with the drummer of Hand Over Fist."

He looks confused for a second. "Oh. I think I understand. Did this meeting change your perspective?"

"Yes," I answered. "Changed it. Altered it. Made me like rock music."

The drummer for Hand Over Fist re-entered just then and gave me some obscure hand signal. It looked like he was talking to himself as he moved through the crowded room. He eventually stumbled over to us. "What's shakin'?" he said to us as he pulled out a candy cigarette.

"The Vikings," Shane said. "The Vikings are about to shake."

"Shit, yeah," said the drummer. "I love The Vikings. Have you seen them before? I bet by this time next year they'll be huge. Like playing big jazz festivals and shit."

As the two guitarists tuned up, the singer of the band addressed the crowd. "The reason we're here tonight is to raise money for a water buffalo." The room got quiet. Libby applauded a few claps and stopped. "Thank you," said the singer. "This is a good example of how we can all make something productive happen. We're not the most political band around but we really wanted to play this show when our friend Shane told us about it. He was a sponsor for a kid who died last month and told us

*creamy bullets*

about him. His name was Raul. He liked soccer, his grandparents, and his bow and arrow. He was a normal kid and he was punished by fate, by global catastrophes, by the imbalance of food and power in this world." I glanced at Shane to see his reaction to this speech. It seemed like everyone was looking his way. He looked tense, holding his breath, a tear ready to drop.

The singer swallowed hard, pausing for his own emotions to calm. "If Raul had a water buffalo this never would have happened. He would have prospered. He would have learned more skills. He would have grown into a man. And maybe he would've come to America and live with Shane or raised his own family. He might have become a famous soccer player." The crowd started to tune him out a little. The singer's sentiment was getting carried away. He shouted over the din. "This is for Shane. This is for Raul. This is not for America." The drums, guitars, horns, keyboards all started blasting then. There were eight people crammed on the stage. Most of them wore Viking helmets. I saw Libby cover her ears and retreat to the back of the room. Her face looked caked with tears. I realized that I was also crying. From happiness or sadness, I wasn't sure. I let the swoop and blur of The Vikings' music wash over me, hit me in the gut, and squeeze my heart. Fifteen minutes later, at the end of the first song, Libby and Shane were standing beside me, their arms around each other. My head felt like it was shaved clean and then grew more hair and then was shaved again. By the end of the set, I felt like I was surrounded by hair, and it was sticking to me by tears or sweat. Libby grabbed me by the jacket, pulled me toward her, and stuck a water buffalo pin on my chest.

I went outside and sucked in some fresh air. I waited to see if Shane and Libby would want to go to the Black Bear or somewhere else to drink. They came out holding hands and bumping shoulders. I quickly ducked around the corner of the building, then took the long way home. I stopped at a convenience store and bought a carton of chocolate milk and a bag of chips. I sat in a park and listened to my crunching drown out the sound of crickets. I nervously walked through a burned out warehouse and saw three people sleeping in a corner. They looked like a family. I stumbled out of there and made my way through backstreets until I could see my apartment building a few blocks away. As I walked through the 2am darkness, I wondered what time it was in Bolivia. If people were opening their eyes as I closed mine. If they were hungry. If they had hope.

# The Show

The curtain opens and there are four people sitting in folding chairs, looking uncomfortable. I am the actor, moving my mouth at them. My body drains of any momentum it may have had going into the show. I feel let down.

I kept telling myself before the show: It's okay if there's not a big turnout...It's a small theater...The show will have an intimate charm.

But the four people do not look charmed.

I try to decide if I should interact with the audience or if I should keep them separated from the character I'm playing. The fourth wall as they call it. I am the only one on stage for the whole show, except for the scene where the old lady comes out and mops the floor in front of me. It is a serious show. A show about the United States.

Afterwards, I spend an hour putting everything away before going to a friend's birthday party. When I arrive there, she tells me that I'm still five years older than her. I drink coffee, while everyone else is careless and drunk.

The next night, there are thirty-five people in the audience. When the performance is over they all clap their hands enthusiastically and I feel a renewed optimism about the upcoming eight shows.

*Hey you, nice message. This is Jackie from the theater. There's been a slight mix-up with the scheduling. I'm afraid you'll have to do your show in ten straight nights, rather than five weekends. I forgot that we had those magicians from Spain coming in a couple of weeks. I hope this doesn't mess you up too much. And remember to leave your rent check in the office on Thursday.*

The third night is a Sunday and seven people sit in the audience. All but one of them is holding a bible in their hands. I am distracted and shamefully edit myself by not saying words like "Shit" and "Lesbian". The old lady who mops the floor on stage while I do the monologue about Florida is nowhere to be seen. I try mopping while still doing the monologue but I slip and fall. All seven people laugh at me. I don't improvise well and soon they are cursing and spitting on me. The one without the bible however, is a friend of mine, and he calls 911 on the outside phone.

*If you need more chairs,* the woman points out to me, *there is a door here to the basement. And when you're done, everything is expected to be as clean as you found it. Here is the key. Lock both locks, and give us a rental check by Thursday. Also understand that there is no drinking allowed inside.*

Nobody shows up on Monday night. There are six more nights of the show and I think about canceling them. I've been feeling sick all day and I've thrown up twice. This may be due to the previous night when I inadvertently swallowed someone's spit. I walk down to the corner store and buy some champagne. Back at the empty theater I drink on the edge of the stage while listening to a New Age CD that someone left by the sound board. Someone opens the door around midnight but I tell them that the show is over.

There is a sign on the theater door when I get there at 6:00 Tuesday. THIS SHOW HAS BEEN MOVED TO 10th AVENUE STUDIOS. I go to the 10th Avenue Studios and there is a line of about eighty-five people. I become nervous and agitated about this sudden change.

I go through the back doors and there are a dozen people running around, looking for me. I am overwhelmed. Usually there is only myself, a lighting person, and the old lady, who also takes the money at the door. I raise my hand and they hurry me out to the stage, telling me where exactly to stand and what kind of facial expressions I should use. Then, crouched over like tennis ballboys, they scuttle off to the side of the stage and the curtains open. All the seats are filled, but it is not even time for the show to begin.

As I begin my performance, the old lady comes out with the mop. I give her a curious, almost angry look. She is blocking my focus on the audience. I maneuver to one side, then the other. I hear a few people chuckle, and I notice that the old lady is really hamming it up with the mop, almost dirty dancing with it, stroking the handle, straddling it, smiling eyes closed in the lights.

I look over to stageside and the people who took me out on stage are smiling, nodding their heads briskly, upper teeth biting their lower lips in glee.

The audience is loving the lady's dance and my words are buried in the din of catcalls and stamping feet. I walk over to the men at stageside and one of them hugs me, while the other musses my hair like an uncle. *That was great*, the uncle-type says to me, *this is just what the show needs. Somebody to play off your straight man. Some kind of Jerry Lewis.*

I try to tell them that it's my show. I wrote it, I'm in it, I'm directing it. They are too busy laughing to hear me.

For the rest of the night I must perform while the old lady dances suggestively and makes lewd remarks to the audience. At first I am angry and then I somehow get caught up in the chaos and start to really play up the new "straight man" role. The men at stageside give me the thumbs up and slap their knees.

*Hello, this is Jackie from the theater. We heard about the show the other night and we decided we'd rather not be associated with people like you. We'd like the rent check and the key today.*

The sixth and seventh nights are much the same. I feel somewhat betrayed the way the show has changed so much but I am at least making the rent money. One of the director guys even cuts pictures of me out of the newspaper review and puts them on the ticket booth window.

On both of these nights we receive standing ovations, and one person tells me they think I'm doing a good job with my monologues, even though she calls them poems and lyrics. One of the directors overhears the person say this to me and says, *That's it! Why don't you write stuff that rhymes and we'll get a drum machine and some hip hop guys. We can get rid of the old lady and do the show for another month.*

Friday night is show #8 and someone has set up about fifty more chairs. Halfway through the show there is an explosion behind me. It is a shower of fireworks of some kind. The audience is dazzled and several people ooh and ahh. There is loud music and several people in giant cat suits bound onto the stage. The old lady seems alarmed as well and begins beating them with her mop. She is collectively booed and, at the end of the show, she is fired from the last two nights.

I go to her dressing room and help her gather her belongings. She is crying and leaning on me. I brush her hair slowly and hold her. She pushes me away and looks down at my pants. Her face is hard and pale as she slaps me.

*That's real classy there, Desmond. Now, keep in mind that the guy is talking about Florida, and the drum is super-bassy, so really gyrate your middle there, like you haven't had any pussy for weeks. Act like you're one of the 2 Live Crew. Yeah, yeah, make it jump out.*

◄ *creamy bullets*

*Now Lisa, change your face more often. Grit your teeth. Do some pain, do some pleasure. Pretend you're with all these hot black guys showin' their underwear and their caps on backwards. You gotta get nice and hot for that final scene with all the tattoo guys. They're not going to be very happy if you're not warmed up. Let's see some of that UCLA technique.*

The curtain opens on Saturday night and I'm exhausted. Two more nights to go and I feel like putting myself on auto-pilot but I know that I need to end the show's run strongly. A short, Chicano girl named Lisa has taken the old lady's role, but we have not rehearsed at all together. *Just go with it*, said the two guys at stageside, *things will be great; Lisa's a natural.*

When I start to speak my voice seems louder than normal. Some kind of synthesized drumbeat begins fading in and Lisa begins to shed her clothes until she is wearing what looks to be an aerobics outfit. Four men appear on the stage, walking menacingly toward her. I try to focus on my words, hiding my concern for her. I shift my body to see the director guys nodding and smiling, letting me know that things are fine.

Lisa does some kind of karate-style move and the men fall in line behind her, dancing a choreographed routine. All five of them smile and display an energetic happiness. The audience starts moaning derisively and some even throw up their hands and leave the theater. Lisa and the dancers become more lewd and aggressive with their movements but the audience has already given up on the show and within minutes the theater is empty.

The men at stageside act as if they don't know me when I walk over to them. Then one of them says, *You blew it, man! You acted like you didn't know what to do. What's wrong with you.*

The other one just pats me on the back and musses my hair, *It's okay*, he says, *keep yourself together. Just one more night and it'll all be over.*

*Just over an hour ago, following a sold-out show, a suspected arson fire broke out and engulfed the 10th Street Theater. Officials say there have been bodies found inside the theater but details are sketchy. People at the neighboring Wilson Hotel were evacuated immediately. Police say there are no suspects at the moment but the few clues gathered thus far do indicate an arson fire…*

A friend calls me that night. He has seen the story on the news and wants to make sure I'm not among the dead bodies. I have no idea who the dead bodies could be. There is a message pinned to my door on

Sunday morning. It's from somebody telling me that the last night of the show would be at the smaller theater it was originally at. I am surprised at first, then happy, realizing that Lisa and the director guys must be okay if we're still doing the last night.

There is a long line for the show when I get there at 6:30. I am grabbed by two women in leather jackets and hurried into the back door. They give me some pills to take and a six-pack of beer. They lock me in a dressing room painted brown. *Everything will be alright,* someone whispers from the other side of the door. *We don't want the police to disturb you, we want you to be fresh.* I eat the pills and drink the beer as I try to relax and go over the show once more in my head.

Two hours later, a sullen man speaking Spanish opens my door and leads me to the stage. As soon as I walk on stage, a large smiling man in a tuxedo grabs my arm and leads me to a giant box at mid-stage. It is on top of a metal platform, with wheels on the bottom. I am puzzled at first, and then I see Lisa standing there. I smile at her. Her hair is blonde tonight and she is a few inches taller. She holds my hand as I get into the box. There is a padded hole at one end to place my neck, so my head sticks out when she closes the top. I start doing my monologue and the audience explodes in laughter as if my voice is the funniest thing they've ever heard. I am flustered and I begin to cry and laugh at the same time. Lisa pushes me down flat into the box. Her arms are more muscular than I remember. I look over to stageside, trying to catch a glimpse of the directors but only see the two women in leather jackets, wearing large hats and holding rabbits in their arms.

The tuxedo man says something in Spanish to the audience. I feel sick as Lisa closes the box over my body. Then the man spins the box around so the audience can see all the sides. The man is addressing them as he does this. Both of his large hands are over my ears, as if he's using my head as a steering wheel. His voice is muffled, ghost-like, foreign. The audience laughs uneasily about something and then becomes very quiet.

I start to feel my legs being pulled, and then quickly a rush of air by my knees. My fingers search in the darkness for what's going on but there is nothing to be found below my knees, just a flat piece of metal where my legs should continue. I wiggle my toes and feel them rub inside my shoes, but they seem far away, on the other side of the stage. I wonder if my feet will live without me.

I hear some people gasping, shifting in their seats. Lisa pushes the part of the box with my legs inside

*creamy bullets*

near my head so I can see what's going on. She takes off my shoe and tickles my feet. I feel it and laugh uncomfortably. She pulls off the sock and kisses my toes. The audience applauds. She pushes the foot into my face and tells me to kiss it. I do. The audience roars with laughter. She pushes that part of the box aside then. The man in the tuxedo pats her on the back pocket of her tight glittery shorts and she moves away. The audience hoots and applauds. Suddenly, his face becomes very serious and he snaps his fingers at Lisa. She brings to him what looks to be an over-sized razor blade. I start trying to push out of the box but it doesn't budge. The audience begins cheering on the man in the tuxedo.

I begin to yell, THIS IS NOT PART OF THE SHOW! THIS IS REAL! But no one hears at all. There is a small slit in the box where my chest is. Lisa helps the man slide the blade in and down. I feel it tearing into my clothes. The audience is in hysterics, hooting and hollering, stamping their feet. The man lifts up a sledge hammer and the volume increases. It becomes deafening when the blood begins to drip out.

# Swimsuit Issue

Guys just stare at my tits without shame. It doesn't matter what I wear. I'll throw something on with a plunge and my whole day is chaos. Every neck cranes freakishly, every eyeball almost popping out like fingers nervously brushing me. The sound of their breathing like an asthma ward. Slow cars cruising beside me. Some of the women have to hold themselves back. They all want to kill me.

At least I can get some service at the hardware store now. Not like ten years ago, when I was going on dates with record store clerks and delivery men—guys who welcomed the non-threatening stature of my small sickly-looking titties. I couldn't even call them tits. I had a child's chest. Titties. A cute name. But mine were horrible and that was why I ended up smashing people's shit. I'd get fed up with everything and I didn't trust nature or God or even my friends.

When I was 28, I somehow ended up with a guy twice my age. My family gave up on me by that point. They didn't even know his name. They just called him *the old guy*, even though his name was simple, strong, standard.

Jack.

He didn't really give a shit about anything. I mean, Jack was really nice but he was a rebel, a man who couldn't be told what to do or think. He made a bunch of money working for some drug company and getting out just before they got sued for clogging up some kid's heart valve or something. They even talked about it on *60 Minutes* and when they tried to interview Jack he just smiled and said he had nothing more to do with the company. The reporter, some black lady with feathered hair poofed out like Farrah Fawcett, asked him something else and Jack stuck his hand out to block the camera and climbed into his Porsche. It was so cool. Sometimes I'll watch that clip on some web site and imagine that I'm there too, in the Porsche, wearing sunglasses and a really expensive dress. And sometimes, yeah, I'll tell people I was there. The camera never gets a good shot into the car.

Besides, I have been in that car. I've been all over that car. I know what the dome light of that car feels like on the bottom of my left foot. I know the perfect way to brace myself against the leather steering wheel. I know the exact position to put the rear view mirror so I can see all this happen. I liked to watch him do it to me, his furry back clenching and sweating. It's why they call it a rear view mirror, I joked to him.

But he hated my titties too. He asked me if I had cancer the first time we had sex. Or at least it seemed like he was asking me that. His face made a horrible face. He screwed me real fast because he wanted to get it over with. His anguish over my body matched my own level of self-hatred. I came despite the hate, or because of it. Then he said I had a pretty face.

I shouldn't say I hate myself. That's not right. I do have a nice face. Cute hair, brown and wavy. My arms aren't gross. I'm thin around the waist and ankles. My ass is actually pretty good. I went to school. I achieved some goals. I type eighty words a minute. I can go a whole weekend alone without killing myself.

So Jack set it up for me pretty quick. Had me quit my job and send the boys to grandma's. I didn't mention my kids yet, did I? Twin boys. Thurston and Lee, eight years old. Good kids, independent, always prowling the neighborhood with those Hispanic kids from down the street. Those little guys are proof that I was once loved by someone my parents approved of. His name was Lesley, like a girl. Won't Lesley be surprised.

It seemed like an eternity later when I could finally remove the bandages. I dragged myself around the halls of the hospital and felt like I was taking someone else's body for a walk. Jack sent me new swimsuits every day while I healed. He said they were actual ones he saw in the swimsuit issue of a sports magazine. He couldn't wait to get me out to the beach.

I'll always remember that moment of the bandages circling off me. I watched in the mirror that the nurse held just right, so all I saw was my middle, now top-heavy, ready to burst forth. It was like watching myself being born again, without a face.

It's amazing what boobs can do. It feels so weird to even say that word in regards to myself. I always used it when talking about others. Ashley's boobs. Naomi's boobs. Someone once said, *If they don't bounce, they're not boobs*. Now I bounce. Jack liked to see me bounce. He didn't want to go a night without doing something obscene to me after my operation. His enthusiasm cranked up my confidence and helped me grow into my new body. And it did feel like a whole new body. Like my tits had taken over my body.

As soon as my scars healed and I got used to the sheer mass and weight of my breasts—the almost ridiculous presence of them—I emailed an old boyfriend from ten years ago and dropped a hint about my new look. This is someone who jokingly called me "little boy" until I started crying. We went out for a whole year and *only* had doggy-style sex. Sometimes he told me to put a t-shirt on when we did it. I think he gave me my first orgasm.

Steve emailed me back and said he was working in a music store, teaching guitar lessons to kids. He told me he'd send me a guitar if I sent him photos of myself. I looked him up on the Internet and saw that he was still cute. I don't really know what I'd do with a guitar but I wanted him to see me so I asked Jack to snap some pictures of me. I didn't say anything about Steve, though I'm sure he probably wouldn't care. He talked to his old girlfriends and I didn't freak out about that.

They turned out pretty good. In one of them I'm sitting on the edge of bed, leaning over a little, the silicone working its magic, staring straight through the lens like missiles. There's a profile shot where you can really see what a nice job the surgeon did. Jack said we should send that one to the doctor. He could put that one on his business card, Jack said. We took a few in some of my new swimsuits too, and then several in the shower. Jack asked me to soap myself up. I liked touching them for the camera. I felt like I could do anything with them and they'd look good. I sent a couple of the photos to Steve and he wrote back saying they looked *sensational.* He said he wrote a song about me and wanted me to hear it. I asked for his phone number so he wouldn't call when I was with Jack. I was jittery about calling him though, and it took me two weeks to gather the nerve.

He sounded the same as he always did when he answered. Really sweet but with a nasty temper buried somewhere. He asked if I was sending more photos and who took the ones he'd already seen. I lied to him and told him a girlfriend had taken them. Stacey, I said her name was. She had hers done too, I said for some reason. We talked for about an hour. He'd ask about my parents and my kids and my life but the discussion always ended up on my tits. Or *breasts,* as Steve first called them. It took him a few cautious moments to warn up to tits, but then he really enjoyed saying it. What did your parents say about them? What do your kids think about them? Sometimes it was like he was interviewing just my tits.

Finally, he played me his song. He set his phone down next to where he was, picked up his guitar, and started serenading me. He stopped halfway. *Can you hear me?* he yelled down at the phone. Yes, I shouted back. He continued his song. Over the phone it sounded like a fuzzy old radio. Some of the words were hard to make out. There was a part where he said something about my face looking hard or maybe he was saying my face made him hard. I didn't want to ask. By the time he got to the third verse I was able to ignore the terrible melody and focus on the words. They dripped with nostalgia, regret, and horniness. I asked him to sing it again and I touched myself as he did. I couldn't quite bring myself off but it was enough for me just knowing that he wanted to have sex with me again.

The next day, he sent me an email saying that he was *thrilled, maybe too thrilled,* to have talked to me. He wrote a description of the kinds of photos he wanted me to send next and asked if he could see a photo of my friend Stacey as well. I responded and told him Stacey wouldn't do it. He sent me a snippy reply, one that was rude and all business. Something like:

*Talk to Stacey some more and tell her I'll make it worth her while. And send me some photos of you with your wig.*

I had told him, while on the phone, about buying a wig after the operation. I didn't say anything about Jack wanting to see me with long blonde hair. I didn't say anything about Jack at all. I said something dumb like, *I'm just into having fun now.* To him it probably sounded like, *I'll hump anything with a penis.* Anyway, I just so happen to have a couple of wig shots. I sent them to him. I titled the email: Say Hello to Your New Blonde Goddess.

After that, Steve insisted on calling the blonde me by a different name. Letecia.

I started to have panic attacks and stopped emailing with Steve. Jack was getting more possessive and I was starting to worry he'd find out.

One night at dinner, Jack said he wanted to get me liposuction. Imagine yourself with fifteen pounds chopped off, he said. You'd be a knockout. I thought it was a weird thing to talk about at dinner but I was happy. I knew that if Jack was spending that kind of money on me it meant that he really loved me. He wanted to make it easy on me and I felt my heart swell and lift. I felt like I couldn't breathe for a moment and when I saw tears form in his eyes, I started crying too. I touched his face and he leaned forward into my hand. He moved to kiss me and his hands moved over my breasts so gently. My *breasts.* I don't mind that word right now, at this moment. It seems right and pure. They were warm to his touch. Always warm.

But the next morning, I realized that I didn't want another surgery. I looked over at Jack as he slept. He had wrinkles, spots, gray bristly hair. Sometimes I forgot what he looked like when he wasn't around. I'd imagine him as a superior being, a master of life, of getting things done. He got things done for me. But what about him? I never noticed that hair growing out of his ears. The weird lines all over his neck. Not wrinkles really, but lines. Like graph paper. I smelled his neck. It smelled like band-aids. My eyes and nose circled his head slowly as he wheezed. Sometimes when he slept he made so much noise it was like he was fighting with someone. There were age spots on his scalp. His hair barely survived there. He was too tan. I wondered if he'd get cancer. I pulled the sheets back and looked down on his body. He had half of a morning hard-on but it was hard to notice under the girth of his belly. His belly button the size of a quarter. I reached over to my purse and took a quarter out. I set it there and it fell inside. For a moment I wondered how far it went. Did it actually disappear in there? Would he carry that quarter around for a few days before noticing it?

I got out of bed quietly. I picked some clothes out of the closet and took off my pajamas. There was a full-length mirror on the closet door. It was a double door, so the mirror was actually in two pieces. In one mirror, I looked at myself naked for a couple of slow minutes. In the other mirror, I watched Jack sleep, the covers pulled down. I wondered if he would wake up if I stared at him long enough. I slowly got dressed, trying to stare at him without blinking. My eyes started to hurt. I finally left the room, closing the door softly. I walked by the boys' room and they were already up and gone. It was a school day. A warm, promising, no clouds in the sky kind of day. I opened the front door and felt the sun on my skin. It lit up my body and I felt good. I slammed the door right then and there.

# Homewreckers

One of the girls next door was getting ready to move out. My wife and I thought they were lesbians but we weren't sure. Sometimes we heard moaning and what sounded like a bed frame quivering and knocking against the wall. They were big girls. Big knocking sounds.

Once I went over to ask them about an ant problem. An invasion. Neither girl was there, but their back door was open. I walked in to find another open door. A messy bedroom with sweat-stained bras slung over the brass doorknobs. Cups bigger than my fists. I listened to the silence whistle as I opened a dresser drawer. Stretched out panties and crisp condom wrappers. I heard a toilet flush.

My wife was doing sit-ups in the front room. She was naked. I entered with her morning coffee. "This is a nice view," I said.

"Thanks," she said.

"For the coffee?" I asked.

She took a sip and leaned her chest on her knees before resuming. "And everything else," she answered.

"Was that you last night? Out here? Making sounds?" I asked.

"No. Fell asleep on couch." Her sentences were short to accommodate her exercise. "Lesbians," she said between huffs.

"Those lesbians like their sounds," I said. I poured some M&Ms into a cup of yogurt and fingered my belly button. The fatter I got, the deeper my inny got.

"The ants are back," she said as she left the room.

"Here's how the ant kingdom works," said James, the maintenance guy. "The worker ants are sent out to find food for the queen. They find crumbs or whatever and take them back to where the queen is. The queen can be a big ol' bitch. Like, up to six inches long." He held out a measured distance between his huge fingers. There was a ring on one of the fingers that looked like it would cut the circulation off.

"You're not serious," I said.

"Oh yeah," he said, eyes getting wide like some UFO chaser. "Those queens can kill a snake or a squirrel."

"A squirrel?"

"Well, I saw one eat a hamster once." He pulled some small plastic circular things from his coat pocket. They looked like miniature models of the Superdome. "These traps have poison and the worker ants get contaminated and go back to the queen ant. The scent of the stuff in these things makes the queen want to breed, so she has sex with a few of her workers and eventually dies."

I couldn't help but imagine a weird ant porno— some tinny techno music playing over a poisonous insect gang bang.

Early morning. Too early to wake up. Maybe before six. A rhythmic thump came through the walls in our bedroom, jarring me from a dream. My wife had fallen asleep on the couch, but now she was up, ready to get in bed with me. Our TV set played a marathon of home improvement shows in the front room. I tuned my ears to the dull clunking, hoping I could hear voices or at least a sharp muffled scream or something. My sense of hearing was good in the dark. My penis was getting hard.

"What are you doing?" my wife asked from the doorway.

"Nothing," I said, eyes half-closed. I nodded at the wall. "Does that sound like lesbian love to you?"

"It's kind of a man's tempo, isn't it?"

The sounds stopped. There were no screams, groans, or exhales. My wife turned on the light. Blankets in a teepee-shape.

A couple weeks ago, James went home for lunch. He lived with his grandmother just a few blocks away from the apartment. She always cooked for him. Brown bag lunch. Most days, I'd see him eating lunch in his truck. But on this day, he ate enchiladas and watched a soap opera with his grandmother. He was supposed to be fixing the water heater in my quad but was behind as usual.

On his way back to work, he passed by a woman who flagged him down. He thought it was someone who needed help. He circled back around the block. On his return, he saw that she was an attractive woman, probably about thirty years old. He rolled the passenger side window down.

"Wanna have some fun?" she asked.

"Yeah. Um. What, uh, what are you doing?"

She fidgeted with the hem of her skirt and leaned over. She looked a little like an old girlfriend of his. "Can I get in? It's hot out here," she said.

James was nervous. He had never been with a prostitute before. He tried to remember what the laws are, the protocol. "Are you a cop?" he forced himself to ask.

"Let me in. I'll show you my pussy. That way you'll know I'm not a cop."

He unlocked the door for her. "I don't see too many girls like you out here," he said.

She got in the car and smiled at him. She lifted her blouse a little and pulled the waistband down on her skirt and panties. Her stomach was a little chubby. "See, I'll show you my pussy. See? I got a cute pussy."

James wanted to reach over and touch it but he just looked. He knew he still had to be careful. What would his grandmother say if this were one of those stings? If he went to jail? He thought if he didn't bring up money, he'd be safe. He hoped she was just a crazy person, a nymphomaniac. "Are you just like a, uh, exhibitionist or something?" When he talked to her it felt like swallowing. Half pride, half greasy air.

"Yeah, that's exactly it," she said. "So, what do you want to do? I could suck you off or we could fuck."

*creamy bullets*

"What do you want to do?" James asked meekly.

"I want to fuck," she said. "I haven't been fucked today."

The neighbor girls sat outside, drinking and smoking as the sun went down. I could see boxes taped up and stacked in the front room. They had moved a few bigger things that day with a U-Haul.

It was hard to tell, really, if they were lovers or sisters or just friends. They looked a lot alike, but one of them had prettier hair. My wife and I never saw them touch. They talked mostly about their friends and said names we didn't know and used combinations of verbs that were unfamiliar to us. Our front door was open and some of their smoke had started drifting in. Suddenly they were yelling at each other.

"You still don't know how to make eggs," shouted the one with nice hair.

"I had a shitty childhood," the other answered.

"You're not a kid anymore."

"Can't I just…"

And then their voices trailed off and hushed.

As they went back inside and closed the door, one of them said, "It's obvious that we all have our weaknesses."

A few hours later, sounds again through the wall. Were they singing to each other?

I even pressed a glass to the wall.

Then, with my free ear, I heard a siren. It got louder. It turned into my alarm clock.

My wife slept on the couch. Wine on her lips.


"I only do this once a week," Molly said to James. She had given him her name, right after she voiced her preference for fucking. "I'm a student," she said. "I just do this to help me pay for school. You have a condom, don't you?"

"No, sorry. Do you?" He wished he could just get to the sex. Just pull over somewhere and pound her in the backseat.

"This store," she pointed. "They sell singles."

He turned a tight corner, scraping and bumping a high curb. He parked in front of the Mini-mart and rushed inside.

There were people standing in line. Someone buying a bunch of lottery tickets. A man on crutches with a case of beer. A woman behind him with a jar of salsa and a newspaper. James looked out the window, saw Molly waiting in his car, looking at something in her lap. He shifted his weight, feeling the swelling of his penis fade against that leg. Molly kept looking up, around. The cashier was slow, maybe actually retarded, mumbling something to the excited lottery ticket buyer. They both laughed. The man on crutches sighed and started to smell like urine and tobacco. James almost forgot what he was in line for. Self-consciously, he let the woman behind him go before him. Molly was smoking in his car. She took the air freshener off his rear view mirror and snuck it in her purse.

My wife was in the kitchen killing ants. Smashing them with a fingertip. I snuck up behind and wrapped around her, cupping her breasts. She ran warm water over her hands as I groped her. "What were you doing at the neighbors?" she asked me.

"When?" I said.

"Yesterday," she said, slipping away from me. "I saw you come out. What's that about?"

"They're lesbians," I said with a hiccup.

"How do you know that? Did you see them doing it?"

"No."

I didn't tell her about the one with pretty hair. I didn't tell her that I saw her crying. I didn't tell her that we talked. That we locked the door.

"What were you doing there?"

"Nothing. I looked around."

I didn't tell her that they were sisters. I didn't tell her about the hug. I didn't feel like telling her about how it felt. The soft body that let my fingers press in. Her name was Jodi. I let it stay in my mouth. We were quiet.

She dried her hands on a kitchen towel. "What would you be looking for?"

"Ants," I said. "I wondered if they had problems too."

James was breathing heavy, trying to explain to his grandmother. He was sitting on the couch. She was in her big rocking chair. "It was Dad's old girlfriend, Denise. She'd babysit me when I was eight or nine and tell me these stories about how she used to be a prostitute. The kind of things she'd have to do. It was weird. They were like adventure stories. I kind of liked them. Every time she'd talk about getting into someone's car, I'd imagine it like a kidnapping. Like she had to escape. Mostly it was about the escape, getting to the end of the adventure, walking away with the money. Dad didn't know she told me these stories. She also told me that was how she met Dad. When Dad was still with Mom."

The TV was still on in front of them, the volume on zero. James sighed. He felt his words tainting the room, the photographs on his grandmother's mantel, the chairs, the brown carpet. He couldn't stand to look at his grandmother just then. His eyes went out of focus on the TV, blurry images that had no place in this private moment. His throat felt like it was closing, or flooding with sickness.

"She showed me things," he continued. "She showed me her female parts."

He heard his grandmother moaning softly. Tears came to him.

"Dad told me later that she was crazy. He said Denise didn't have any friends to talk to. But it was weird. Because I liked her more than most people. So I thought we were friends. She told me secrets and I saw something amazing in that. Dad never told me anything. There was nothing for us to share. When Denise left I wanted to go find her, but I wasn't even old enough to drive yet. When I was old enough, I couldn't bring myself to drive to that part of town. I couldn't approach a woman like that. I always hoped that Denise or someone like her would find me, that they would pick me out."

He closed his eyes and felt his cheeks get wet. He covered his face and took a deep breath before he went on. "I'm just scared that I'll like it too much. Already, I feel like a different person."

Outside the front door came the sound of his grandmother's cat fighting with a neighborhood cat.

James got up to open the door. He called for the cat. He was glad for this distraction. He looked up and down the street, moving his stiff neck. He breathed in the outdoor air. The cat sprinted around a corner and ran into the house. It leaped into the rocking chair with James's grandmother. She woke from her sleep, startled.

The sounds were happening again. I had just fallen asleep and now I was wide-awake again. I wanted to pound on the wall but held myself back. I tried to reason with myself. They were surely nice girls. They probably didn't know they were making so much noise. I looked over at my wife who was still sleeping, mouth half-open and wet in the corners, eyelids twitching, one arm flopped over her head as if waiting for a teacher to call on her. I climbed out of bed and put some sweats on. As I was walking out the back door by the kitchen, I saw a swarm of ants on the counter hauling away big crumbs of cheese and Ritz crackers. I took some paper towels and wiped them into an open paper bag. I made sure to get them all, even as they tried climbing out of the bag. I could almost hear them calling out or screaming. From the bedroom, the knocking became louder and faster. I went outside with the bag. I cased the apartments, trying to see anything. Through one of their windows, I was able to see around the curtains and into the bedroom. The girl with pretty hair was lying there, reading a book. I couldn't see anyone else. It was quiet. Before I went back into my apartment, I put the bag of ants on the sidewalk and lit it on fire. After all the popping and hissing and smoke, I heard the banging again, coming from the bedroom.

The next morning, Jodi came over to ask us if we could "possibly be quieter when it's late at night." I didn't know if she was joking or being angry. My wife laughed and told her that we were going to ask her to do the same. Jodi glared at me in disgust. My wife stopped laughing. We all stood there, thinking. I went to call James.

James arrived with a canister of ant poison and a tool belt, heavy with blunt objects. "There's a way we can get in over here so that it doesn't actually damage your walls." He led Jodi, my wife and myself to a place in the basement. "Sometimes we get varmints down here," he said.

I wasn't sure if he was totally serious about that. I thought *varmints* was a made-up word that country people used.

"Whatever it is might be more active at night because that's when it gets quiet. It might be sleeping right now," said James. "We've had raccoons before. So it's possible that I may have to call someone else down here if that's what it is." He jostled open a small door that I guessed would place him somewhere under our bedroom. He turned on a large flashlight. "Stand back on that bench," he said, pointing behind us. We scuttled back and stood on the bench. The basement was full of other tenants' storage and some maintenance equipment like saws and pipes and paintbrushes. Someone had a warped pool table leaning against one wall, next to a taped-up poster of some teen girl singer I didn't recognize.

James stuck his head and shoulders into the square space. It looked like it was big enough for one person to crawl into if needed. I wondered if anyone ever stuck a dead body in there. James poked his head back out and coughed. He wiped at his eyes and spit on the ground. "Shit," he said, and stuck his head back in.

We all watched him and started to get a little concerned. "Is it safe to do that?" my wife called out. James stayed there, emerged a few seconds, then braced his foot on the wall and pushed himself up further. All we could see now was his left leg, dangling out of the dark hole. A brief rustling sound was heard. After a minute, he lowered himself back out.

"It's right where you said it was," he said to all of us. He stood there like he was trying to think of something else to do. "Come look," he said, pointing just at me.

I walked over and scanned his eyes for clues as to what it might be. "It's okay," he said. "She's a sound sleeper."

I looked back to my wife and saw a look of jealousy, as if she wanted to be the one looking in this darkness and between the walls. She turned to Jodi and said, "Men are so stupid." I could tell she was just trying to provoke.

"Let the men get dirty," Jodi answered. "They all like to get dirty."

I stuck the flashlight in ahead of me. It didn't seem like dirt up there really. More like a rough cement gutter, leading to tufts of sharp pink insulation. There was more room between the walls than I expected. After climbing a little further up I saw some movement. At first I thought it was a tail but quickly realized it was a trail of ants, an inch-thick army leading into a larger opening. I felt my feet searching for leverage and pushing against the wall under me. I tested a pipe for its temperature before grabbing it and pulling myself all the way up to see into the opening.

My eyes loomed wide and unblinking on the scene. There were dusty ant carcasses all over the place, males with wings torn half-off and heads smashed gruesomely. In the middle of all this was the queen ant, the egg layer. She was about the size of my hand, sprawled—as much as you can imagine an ant being sprawled—on a mound of sandy-looking dirt. She didn't move or even flinch, even with a couple of males copulating with her huge thorax. One winged male fluttered softly around her head, also eager to mate.

I began to smell a brew of scents that arose from the busy colony. First lemons, then the musty smell of cheddar popcorn, then burned toast.

Some of the ants were fighting to get to the queen, crawling over others until they too could clutch her thorax for a few valuable seconds.

"Is everything okay?" I heard someone ask. Either Jodi or my wife.

The queen ant stirred a little then and she began twitching. It looked as if a number of eggs were expelling from her abdomen and oozing forth. Many of the males mated with her aggressively even as she did this. Here is where I noticed the knocking sound. It banged and echoed in the space where I was. I tried to cover my ears and noticed the queen leaning forward with her head pointed at me. I thought I could make out the eyes, golden green. It looked as if she were bracing herself or thinking. I stared back weakly, and for the first time, felt like an intruder.

# Krystal

The number four most requested song began playing. Conner had three and a half minutes to talk on the phone. "When does she have to go back to the doctor?" he asked her.

"Next Monday," she said. "That'll be your day. Plus I'll need your half for daycare. So you owe me three hundred and sixty dollars now."

"Okay. I'll get it to you by next Wednesday when I drop her off."

Conner pressed the button on the switchboard and his ex-wife's voice ceased in his head. He turned up the sound in his headphones and tried to nudge himself into some sort of rhythm that would shake his mind from his troubles. He often found that if he let his body swell with the music while he worked his night shift, the problems in his head subsided or at least were clouded over momentarily. He called the weather line quickly to get the current numbers before the song faded out. He popped in the weather bumper and hit the button that triggered its dramatic intro: Portland-Portland w-w-w-w-weather!

"Fifty-eight degrees on a sweet Thursday night. Expect it to be a little cooler tomorrow, with a high around sixty-six. You keep asking for it, we keep giving it to ya', here's the newest from Ricky Martin; the third-most requested on the Killer, KKLR." He had three minutes and sixteen seconds. He answered phones.

Conner wasn't surprised anymore about the immaturity of his audience. They had thin, frail voices like rubber squeak toys and could barely pronounce the word "request". Once in a while he would get into these awkward conversations with lonely teen-age girls. These were his radio groupies.

They were girls barricaded in their houses by their controlling parents. Girls who found it easier to talk on the phone or send e-mails rather than talk with people face-to-face, body-to-body, insecurity to insecurity.

"You've called the Killer."

"Can I ask you something?"

"Sure. Whaddaya want to hear?"

"What?"

"What song would you like me to play?"

"No. I mean, I just wanted to ask you if you knew something."

"Okay. What is it?"

"Is Ricky Martin gay?" The voice belonged to what sounded like a 13-year-old white girl trying to sound black. Conner turned to look at one of the posters of the Latin pop star that hung throughout the station.

"Well, he does wear leather pants that lace up in the front. That's serves as a clue for me."

"So, will you guys stop playing him if he turns out gay?"

"No. I don't think that's a factor anymore. Ever hear of Elton John?"

"Who?"

"Never mind."

"Are you gay or something?"

"No. Sorry to let you down."

"My dad says that Conner Cavanaugh sounds like a gay name."

Conner sucked a strawfull of Mountain Dew in his mouth and let the taste seep into his tongue. "I think some uncles on my dad's side of the family leaned that way but their name was Litswick."

"Huh?"

"Did you want to request a song?"

"Do you have a girlfriend?" Her sentence seemed to be punctuated by a drag on a cigarette.

"No. I'm too young," he lied.

"Yeah, right. I bet you're like forty years old and married."

Conner twisted in his chair, putting things that looked like old eight-track tapes into the machines around him. He pushed a button and an electronic voice said, "Portland's non-stop music station. The K-K-K-K-Killer." The second most requested song started with no music, just vocals. Some country music singer doing the crossover into pop.

"I hate this guy," the girl on the phone said. "All those country music people are racists."

Conner thought about responding to that but learned from previous experience that it was useless to argue with a teen-ager. "So, what's your name?" he asked.

"Why, are you going to ask me out on a date?"

"No. No, no, no."

"You're not going to ask me out?"

Conner tried to think of something clever to say, something that would leave that option open. She did sound kind of cute. He let out a short noncommittal huff.

"Well, my name is Kristy, but my friends call me Krystal."

Conner wrote her name down so he wouldn't forget. He thought of Crystal Methamphetamine.

*creamy bullets*

He had never done it before because he thought it would probably make him delusional. He saw television news shows that talked about people who thought they could fly or people who could be hit in the face with a hammer and not feel it because they were on the drug. *Did he just see that on TV?* Maybe he saw that when he was a kid. They were more freaked out by drugs when he was a kid.

"So, where are you calling from, Krystal?"

"Southeast. Out by Oregon City. Where do you live?" It had come out so quick, so smooth that it caught Conner a little by surprise. Was she making a move?

"I live out that way too. In that area around 82nd. All those used cars."

"You ever go to that paintball place? The Battlezone?" she asked him.

Paintball. He'd thought about playing it when it first became popular but none of his friends wanted to. Who played paintball anyhow? Teenagers? War veterans? Jocks? Lawyers? Was it cool?

He cleared his throat. "I haven't been there before. Do you go there?" he asked.

"I've only done it once but I go there sometimes with my brother and just play the video games."

"Only played once, huh?"

"Yeah, it's such a jock thing. These guys were shooting at my tits."

"Nice." He immediately felt weird saying that. He realized he had to get ready for the next song. "Hey, hold on a second, okay?"

He pushed a button and brought up his mic volume. "Here it is. For the third night in a row. The most requested song on the Killer." A glassy computerized drumbeat pounded and a pair of rappers began to rap so fast over the beat it almost made the need for it unnecessary. Conner could barely understand every other word. *Slang slang slang beep/slang slang slang beep beep...*

"I love this song," Krystal said when he punched her line back up.

"Yeah, well. There's actually a couple of other songs on their CD that are a lot better," he said. *Was he sounding too snobby for her?* "I mean, yeah. It's a cool song though."

It sounded like she laughed a little, or sighed, or yawned. "Do you want to meet me at the Battlezone this weekend? I mean, I'm going to be there, like, with a couple of friends and stuff. They would think it's cool to meet you."

He lingered near the change machine with a couple of crisp dollar bills in his hand. It was just past two in the afternoon and the place was crowded. He had no idea how he would tell her from the others. He saw a couple of girls that he wished were her but knew they probably weren't. She told him that she looked a little like Julia Roberts but she was half-Mexican and not as skinny. That could have meant anything. Sometimes he looked in the mirror and saw Sean Penn looking back. Or Sean Penn's chubby brother. It depended on his mood.

One girl came up and asked him for a cigarette. He didn't want to give her one but he did anyway, just to try and talk with her. "Do you know a girl named Krystal?" he asked nervously.

"Oh sure," she said, snapping her gum and lighting her free Marlboro. "Go over to the bathroom and pretend you're watching the battles on the TVs."

He was going to question her but he already felt stupid. He was probably getting involved with another high school freshman. He watched the girl as she weaved through the kids, supposedly to find Krystal.

There was a big monitor near the bathrooms so anyone could watch some of the paintball battles going on in the other part of the huge old building. The screen was divided into four sections and he watched a variety of wild-eyed cavemen slumping through and sometimes little kids as well, paint splattered and limping with grimaces on their faces. He looked for any females doing battle but had no luck. He painfully felt the need to see a woman with paint splattered on her chest.

"You want Crystal?" a young man next to him said. Conner looked over and saw a tall teenager wearing a mesh T-shirt and baggy jeans. The young man had a buzz-cut and his hands dug so deep and recklessly in his pants that Conner could see his pubic hair poking out, red and gangly. Pushed down any further, the kid's dick would come flopping out.

"I was just supposed to meet Krystal and some of her friends," Conner informed him.

"Friends, huh?"

"Yeah, um…do you know the Krystal I'm talking about? Looks kind of like Julia Roberts but a little heavier. Part Mexican."

The teenager laughed viciously, his pants almost falling. "C'mon," he said, and held the door to the bathroom open. No one else was in there. "Here," he said undoing the loose belt on his pants. "This ain't really Mexican but that shit is so bogus anyway. If you want some real imported stuff you should try Canadian." Conner watched as the teenager pulled a bag of powder from the inside of his pants. In the dull bathroom light it looked gray and sand-like.

Conner felt his arm move without him. He grabbed the bag and sensed its weight.

The door swung open and an older man lunged in. He was wearing a white battle suit and it was covered in orange and green paint. "God damn, they got me in the ear! Fucking hearing aid's all fucked. God damn!" The teenager grabbed the two dollar bills out of Conner's hand and darted from the bathroom before the door even closed behind the wounded man. Conner stuffed the bag in his jacket and headed out as well. "Hey! A little help, God damn you! Can I get a little help?!" the splattered man called out.

Conner made his way back to the change machine and looked for the girl he had given the cigarette to. He wasn't quite sure what just happened in the bathroom. Was he daydreaming? He thought that since he had to pay so much attention to everything at work that sometimes he spaced off when he was out doing other things. Once, he took his daughter to the park to play and as he sat on a bench, his little girl, then three years old, wandered too close to the skateboarders and accidentally got hit. Her arm was broken and she had to wear a tiny pink cast for three weeks.

"Hey, are you the DJ?"

Conner looked at a young girl whose resemblance to Julia Roberts was nowhere to be found. "Hey. Krystal?" he asked.

"I can't deal with this place anymore. Let's go for a ride or something."

As they walked outside, Conner felt a nervous surge heating up around his armpits. She looked like she could be eighteen and she was actually pretty attractive. Like Roseanne Arquette in *Desperately Seeking Susan*. He felt a pliable energy around her, as if he could eventually have his way with her, sooner not later.

Conner held the door of his Rabbit open for her. He started it up and the squall of an old hard rock song slipped out of his stereo until he turned it down. As they were pulling out of the parking lot, the tall teenage boy who had given him the bag in the bathroom came rushing up to his window. "Hey buddy. Hey. Hey!" Conner pulled out into traffic and tried to pretend he didn't know the kid. He turned up the radio again but could still hear the yelling. "You only gave me two dollars!"

"I know who that guy was," she kept saying as they drove. Conner was going to take her to his apartment but he was driving in a strange roundabout pattern, hoping she would not remember how to get to his place. She kept jabbing him and smiling weirdly, like they'd known each other for a long time and she knew when he was hiding something. "I know you got something from that guy," she said.

"I don't know who that guy is. You tell me," Conner finally said, trying not to smile too much.

"Let me see what you got from him."

Conner pulled out the bag and placed it gently in her lap. He tried to gauge her reaction. "Pull over right here," she said anxiously. They pulled up next to a closed barbershop. "This looks like the same stuff I had last weekend. Good fuckin' shit."

Conner didn't want to ask what it was. He was cool enough to have it, wasn't he? Why blow his cover now? He thought for a few seconds that maybe he should become more of a druggie. Especially if it meant getting to mess around with Arquette-look-a-likes and watching old army vets have their hearing aids blasted out by paintball psychos. She pulled out a popsicle stick and wet it with her tongue. She brought up a perfect mountain-shaped lump and snorted it up her flexing nostril. She licked the rest off and passed the stick to him. *What happened to using straws?*

He looked around quickly and then took a little onto his tongue. It tasted like shit. "Snort it," she said. He hadn't snorted anything before. He tried a smaller mountain for his nostril but exhaled as he brought it up and it blew off, falling dust-like onto his pants. She smiled a little and her eyes looked red. "Out of practice?" she said playfully. Conner looked down at his pants and started to brush it off. "No, wait," she said. She leaned over and put her face near his lap. She sucked it up gently, little snoring sounds escaping the back of her throat. She sat up straight then and tilted her head back a little. "Clean pants," she said.

As he was finally pulling up to his apartment building, she started to play with her hair nervously. "I'd rather go to my place," she said.

"Oh, do you have your own place?" Conner asked. "I mean, we don't want to piss someone off if we're going to do this stuff." He was into doing whatever she wanted but he was feeling strange about driving. It seemed like he was going so much faster than everyone else and his little Rabbit was feeling like a Cadillac. He was suddenly low to the ground in the thing. His ass was almost touching the asphalt and his feet hovered over his body instead of on the pedals. They were being pulled by a cable connected to the power lines. *Yeah*. He was a fucking bus driver!

"I need more and I just want you to come to my place anyway," she said. "I'm only about ten blocks from here."

Conner drove the ten blocks, which turned into sixteen blocks and felt like fifty, his car like one of those long drag racing vehicles, except wobbling through space. The parachute billowing behind them, shadowing their bodies. He was almost embarrassed about the parachute.

"I'm not Krystal," the girl said. "I'm just the bait."

What? Conner felt something disconnect in him, his brain lost. "What is Krystal? Who is Krystal?" he said, and laughed uneasily. Some of the drug was out on a plate on a low wooden coffee table in front of him. He sat directly in the middle of the leather couch, staring at it and trying to estimate how long he was going to be messed up.

"Krystal's my mom," she said.

Conner groaned and rested his head on his shoulder. The girl came over and caressed his cheeks. She leaned against him and he opened one eye to see down her thin red shirt. It was like a doily and it glowed burgundy on her chest, her orange nipples.

More powder in his nose.

His weekend was over. Where had it gone? He hadn't even found time to call his daughter or his daughter's angry mother. Instead, he seemed to be watching things happen to him in slow motion. Things he couldn't stop or for some reason he didn't care to stop. He was in a clean room now, a woman's room.

In a bed. There was an older woman next to him. They were both wet with sweat and other moisture. The woman was most likely in her 50s, old enough to have veins everywhere he looked. To have teeth that didn't seem real. Teeth that seemed to dangle over him as she rode him in an unsteady manic rhythm. The woman did everything she could do to him, pushed him into every part of her. She pressed his chubby belly with her own swollen breasts. She worked him like a chore. Until she was done.

Conner stumbled out of the apartment as another morning started somewhere on the calendar. Did he have to be at work tonight? Or did he have one more day? He had to find a newspaper or something. A friendly stranger? *"Excuse me, can you tell me what day it is?"* What did he think he was, a hostage?

He enjoyed himself anyway, or at least he thought he probably did. He thought about the man with the hearing aid shot out, shouting for help and God damn. The white suit splattered with paint. It was a disgrace. An embarrassment. A pathetic attempt at sport that turned into pleading. A bad game that turned worse.

# The Layover

I walked nervously behind him, into the harsh white surroundings of the men's bathroom at the Dallas airport. I'd never seen a place so bright and clean.

I followed him in there. He turned around when the door closed and this look came on his face, like the brightness hurt. He squinted a slow 360 before looking at me sideways.

"You want to go into town first? Go on a little date?"

I walked over to the sink and splashed my face with water while trying to figure out what my answer would be. I rubbed the bubble gum-scented soap into my right eye by accident. I looked down at my shoes, which were falling apart. I had a layover. Twelve hours.

"Yeah, we can do that I guess."

We drove into Dallas and I was startled at how big and metropolitan it was. I always thought it would be ugly and full of cowboy hats. His car cruised like slow motion through a part of town that was scattered with drug dealers and women pretending to talk on pay phones. I tried not to think about Rhonda or John.

"You say, Hey baby, and if he acts like he's paying attention to you then you say, You workin'? That's about it. Let him lean in the window so we can take a good look. Tell him you aren't a cop, but don't say anything about money because *he* might be a cop. Let *him* tell you how much his dick is worth."

He seemed to know this wasn't my scene, but he said it didn't matter. He liked to break in new ass. And he liked to suck a boy's cock as he did it. He'd get bored with just one guy.

"Where's your wife?" he asked me, spotting the ring on my finger.

"She lives in Eugene, Oregon. She works at the—"

"You got kids with her?" he interrupted.

"One."

"You think he might be gay?"

"He's only ten," I said.

"Does he look at porno yet? Like hard core stuff?"

"Never found any in his room before," I told him. "But when I was his age I think I was into really big tits. Raquel Welch and Dolly Parton. The whole mother's milk thing."

"You should try boy nipples more—not so flabby," he informs me.

"My wife is flat-chested," I said to him. "Sometimes I think she's a boy. I bought her a fake mustache once. I fell in love with her mouth. Her mouth and her skin."

"You tell her you pick up on men?"

"I told her about things in the past. She even slept with one guy I did once and we talked about his tattoos. She wanted me to get a tattoo down there."

The next morning I woke up at his place and realized I missed my flight by several hours. I got up and looked for a telephone to call the airport. A handsome black boy, about 17, was putting on a coat and opening the door. He gave me an uneven, nervous grin and slipped out of the apartment.

"You don't even know my name," a voice said.

I looked over and saw the man from the airport, standing in the bathroom doorway.

"You can call me Jeff," he said, smirking.

"I've missed my plane," I told him, looking for my shoes.

"It's okay. I saw your tickets. I called and postponed for you. I thought you'd want to rest after last night. In fact, you should probably just stay in bed."

He walked over to me let his towel fall away, his washed cock half-hard and swaying there. "I just shaved it," he said, "Smell the Winto-green?"

I did, and almost gagged from the air around us.

"There's some water and an extra toothbrush all ready for ya," he said, waving toward the bathroom.

While I was brushing my teeth, Jeff said something from the bedroom. I had the water running loudly but I think he said: "You fucked my boyfriend last night."

"Something smells queer in here," one of the three men at the bar said when we sat down behind them. Their barstools spun around to face us. "You're not cruising when we're in here, you got that?" His black cowboy hat said CLYDE on the front, the letters arched around an eagle.

The bartender walked over and said something to the men. They huffed and returned to their drinking. They all wore leather and denim in various combinations.

A Kenny Chesney song played on the CD jukebox. Jeff sang along to the chorus and then leaned over to my ear. "The small guy there, with them-" he started to say but was stopped quickly by unwanted eye contact from the bar.

"Why don't you talk so we can hear y'all," Clyde said. The other two kept their mouths closed tight, as if they weren't allowed to speak. Their mouths only opened for beer, with Clyde sometimes rambling on to them in an almost-fatherly tone. I noticed he was the only one in the bar who kept his cowboy hat on. He slid off his stool, boots clicking the floor loudly, and he stumbled a bit as he stepped suddenly toward our table. He seemed to be drunk.

"Okay, okay," he said loudly as if about to make an announcement to the whole bar. His hands went up, palms out. "I got to apologize to ya boys," he said. "This is a public bar and you can do whatcha want to. I've been here long enough anyhow. It's time to get my men back home." The other two got up and pulled their jackets on. Clyde motioned to the bartender. "Get Jiffy and his friend here a beer on my tab."

"Have you lived in Texas all your life?" I asked Jeff.

"No, no," he answered, "I grew up in Baton Rouge. Louisiana."

I took a slow drink from the thin watery beer. "When I was a kid my favorite football team was the New Orleans Saints, so I always wanted to live there."

"Louisiana's no place for kids. For strung-out grown-ups maybe and criminals, but for sure not little boys," he said.

"What did you do while growing up there?"

Jeff scooted closer to me and I felt his hand hover over my leg, near my crotch. Despite myself, I had an erection.

"My friend Truman and I, we, like pretended this game. I think we were nine or ten. I'd wear his sister's clothes and hide somewhere in his house. When he found me I'd act all scared and weak. He had a pocket knife." Jeff's hand pressed against my hard-on as he spoke in a steady whisper.

His breath was filling my nostrils. I tried not to breathe. The neon window lights around his head pulsed like a sick halo.

"I'd have to lay on my back when he found me. I didn't wear any underwear and if I did he'd pretend-hit me until I slid them off. Sometimes toward the end of the game he'd let me have the knife and I would rub the dull side along his dick like I was whittling a stick. I'd suck on the head and whittle the rest. The first time I did that he got scared and pissed a little on my chin. I thought it felt pretty good and so then sometimes he'd piss a little bit on

*creamy bullets*

me after he came. He'd wash the sperm off me that way."

I jumped a little as the bartender swept our beer bottles away and replaced them with full ones. He looked at Jeff and smiled knowingly, as if he knew the story being told. I looked at Jeff and saw his strange smile but also something on his cheek, like tears, or maybe just sweat.

Jeff and I spent the rest of the day shopping and sight-seeing. He wanted to buy a pair of women's panties and a bra. "You can give these to your wife when you're home," he said, and I felt some relief knowing that he realized I had to go soon. "What size does she wear?"

At 8:00 that night we began eating dinner back at his apartment. I told him I had made reservations for a flight home at a quarter after midnight.

"I wish I was married," Jeff said. "I mean to a man. I kinda get pissed sometimes because you gotta have a straight marriage to get kids and have a family. Sure, you'll see rich fags and closet-dykes with kids, but not too often middle-class and out of the closet."

We were drinking wine. On the couch were several small bags from our day shopping—toys and books for my son John. A pair of panties and bra for my wife Rhonda, courtesy of Jeff's Visa card. A gift box of assorted cheese and crackers for myself.

"Do you spank your son?" Jeff asked me.

"Once I did when he was four. I didn't want to but I was under a lot of pressure. He was playing underneath our neighbor's police car after I'd told him twice that week not to. I never saw the guy drive it at all. I just saw it there every morning. He worked the night shift. And what's kind of funny is that I never even knew what the guy *looked like* until he died last year and his picture was in the newspaper."

Jeff shifted in his chair, knowing that I was drifting off the subject. "Did you feel love for him as you were doing it? Or anger?" he asked.

"Both, I guess."

"Have you ever hit your wife?" he asked.

I thought for a moment, wondered how the word "hit" was defined in this question. "No. But she hit me once. Drew blood." My finger touched my nostrils lightly. My face felt unreal.

"I want you to be your wife," he said, standing up. He grabbed one of the bags from the couch. He looked at the clock and his eyes went intense.

He bit my nipple through the cloth and pulled the straps down off my shoulders. "I think this looks sexy," he said. I was wearing the bra and panties for my wife. One of his fingers pushed itself into my ass, through the black lace of the panties. It felt good this way, better than just his dry skin.

"Move like your wife would move. Make her sounds," Jeff whispered in my ear. "I want to know what it's like." The toys and books for my son had been taken out of their bags and scattered around near us.

Part of me shut down. I didn't want to pretend this game. I felt mocked in some way. Despite this feeling I became more aggressive. My hand wrapped around his warm cock and I wanted him to get inside me. Two of his fingers were starting to stretch me out, pushing the soft fabric into me.

I felt him get bigger, wider in my hand. He took his hand from my ass and pulled me to my knees. He stood in front of me and told me to squeeze my tits. He rubbed his dick against my cheek. He pulled it sideways and slapped me with it harder than I expected. It stung. He guided it into my mouth. It pressed down on my tongue, taking up all the space between my cheeks. I breathed through my nose. I tried to masturbate but he stopped me. "Save it," he says.

His hips pulled back and his dick slid out from between my teeth. I choked for air, trying to work my mouth to say the words I desperately wanted to say to him. "I want you to fuck me. I want—"

His cock sprayed me with cum. Some of it in my eyes, on my face, down my neck and chest. And then a last shot in my open mouth. He grabbed my head and softly nuzzled it against his chest and belly. We stuck together awkwardly.

"I know what you want," he said softly. "It might change you forever. Maybe you'll come back to me. Maybe we could be a family."

The clock said 10:25pm and my body still twitched with a pulsing erection. I tried to keep him hard with my hand.

"If I'm the first to fuck you, would you fall in love with me like a schoolgirl?"

I looked at his face and drifted into his eyes. I lusted.

"Do you understand what I'm about to give you?" he asked me.

# Cat in Residence

At night, when my wife and I are together at home, we get into our "Night Uniforms." Her Night Uniform is usually baby blue sweats, long sleeve thermal shirt, and a black hoodie. My Night Uniform is being nude. There are some variations to my Night Uniform though. If I keep my socks on it's called The Lewd Uniform. If I keep my socks and a T-shirt on it's called The White Trash Uniform. We keep our blinds shut tight.

Most of the time, we stay up until midnight, changing into our Night Uniforms often as early as 8pm. We sit on the couch, zoning out to the television and drinking decaf coffee. We're not a very talkative couple but we're relaxed in our own way. My legs tuck themselves under Annie's and she'll read magazines during the commercials.

On other nights, we walk around the neighborhood looking for cats to play with. Our street is full of them. We don't have our own pets because we travel too much. Same thing goes for kids. There's too many things loaded on our blackberries and scribbled in our day planners and not enough time for much else. I run a marketing firm and Annie writes for travel magazines.

Last year, an elderly couple moved into the bungalow apartment next door. They have two cats, a brother and sister that look exactly alike. I saw these animals strolling down the sidewalk outside our kitchen door as I washed dishes. I walked out softly and called to them but they scampered away. Annie told me later that they ran from her too.

Some cats will come right up to you. They'll bow their head and rub against your hand. They'll lay on the ground and stretch out for you. Some will let you pet them once before walking away teasingly and then coming back just as you're about to walk off. Our neighbor's twin short-haired Tabby cats watched us, leery and leaning the opposite direction from us, for quite a while. We put a water bowl on our back porch to show them we wanted to be friends.

Eventually, one of them approached me when Annie was away writing an article on some warm weather resort—her assignments sometimes blurred together for me. He had a nametag that said Baxter. He also had a bell attached to his collar, unlike his sister. He seemed pretty calm as I petted him. I noticed his sister under a parked car, watching us. I took a few steps toward where she was, but she darted away silently. Baxter stayed near me though, and began purring.

"Well, he seems friendly toward you," the old lady next door said. She was outside, smoking on her porch. I had met her once but couldn't remember her name.

"Oh, hi," I said. "What do you call your other cat?"

"That's Bubble," she said, taking a drag. "She's a scaredy-cat."


By the time Annie got back into town, Baxter was drinking water out of the bowl on our back porch and even coming into our apartment for short visits. While Bubble still wouldn't let me touch her, Baxter would roll onto his back and let me rub his belly while playfully attacking my hand. He almost looked like a tiger cub but his legs were mostly white, like he was wearing boots. Whenever Annie cooked meat in our kitchen I'd give Baxter some scraps. Annie shook her head and said we were corrupting the neighbor's cat and that they probably didn't even eat meat. We had started calling his owners "his parents" and just in case his "parents" could hear us talking through the wall, we gave him the secret code name, Mr. Hoo-Ha. But my wife loved the fact that Baxter came inside. It was our chance to pretend we had a pet.

"It makes me feel like we're having an illicit affair with him or something," she said. "His parents go to work, he walks over, and we let him right in. He must have slept on our bed all afternoon yesterday." She didn't really know the full stats. When I was home working alone, Baxter would stay inside our place for at least nine-hour stretches. I was a little surprised about his laziness, and that he didn't get up to eat or look for a place to pee. He'd sit somewhere with his arms and legs tucked under his big round middle. Annie and I called this "Turkey Position" because it made him look like a Butterball.

Only a few weeks after this, Baxter started coming around at night, often running at full speed down the sidewalk when he'd see our car pull up. His bell would ring impatiently as we unloaded groceries from our trunk. We'd let him in and he would go straight for our room. He'd lie on our bed for a few hours while we changed into our night uniforms and watched TV or read. We'd let him out when it was time for us to take over the bed. One night though, he slept on top of our dresser, on a precarious pile of clothes. We didn't notice him there until the morning, when he joined us in bed, laying snug between us, purring loudly.

In the morning, we snuck him out the other door and then made coffee and breakfast for ourselves in the kitchen. "I wonder if Mr. Hoo-Ha's parents knows he comes over here," Annie said. We both imagined scenarios where the neighbors came over and saw Baxter there, eating chicken off the little cat plate we bought him (it had a drawing of a chicken on it). The old woman would be most upset and she would swear loudly and lunge at us like on one of those bad afternoon talk shows. Somebody's shirt would get ripped, a wig would flop off, and maybe a chair would be thrown.

Of course, it became a ritual. Baxter would stay all day at our place if one of us were there. Then he'd go home just long enough to eat and a couple hours later he'd be jingling his bell outside our door. Maybe he liked us because we were younger. Maybe he didn't like living with his sister, Bubbles, who was still wary of us, even though we tried to lure her in with chicken a few times too. Maybe he liked our flannel sheets. We couldn't be sure. I read somewhere that when a cat looked at you through narrowed eyes, it meant he loved you. Baxter had that look sometimes.

When the weather started to get colder, Annie took the opportunity to write a story in the Bahamas. A Tropical Halloween. I had to stay home and write a holiday campaign for a struggling toy store chain. I hadn't seen Baxter for a few nights. I was secretly hoping he'd come and sleep next to me while Annie was away.

As I was getting ready for bed one night, I heard the jingle jangle of Baxter's bell outside the door. I let him in and he went immediately to the couch and jumped on one of the oversized pillows. He sat straight up like a sphinx and seemed more serious than usual. "Hey Mr. Hoo-Ha," I said. "Did you come over for a sleep-over?"

"You better get comfortable," he said. "I think we should talk about a few things."

I can remember this feeling coming over me right then. Not one of shock exactly, but one of secret shame—like he was a dead relative seeing me in my own private moment; Uncle John making a special ghostly trip to tell me how I should have chosen a more noble career. I wasn't about to believe a cat was actually talking to me. "Who...are you?" I asked him quietly. I was somehow still aware that the neighbors might hear me through the walls.

"You know my name," he grumbled. "And it ain't Mr. Fuckin' Hoo-Ha."

I noticed he had a slight British accent and his words sounded as sharp as his teeth. His mouth didn't move like animals that talk in movies. It was fluid and natural, like he'd been practicing in a mirror.

I almost laughed as I blurted several questions at him. I can't even remember what I asked. I just opened my mouth and question marks came out. I felt dizzy and I awkwardly stumbled sideways a little.

"Now just calm yourself down," Baxter told me. "Sit your ass over here. We got shit to talk about."

I made it a point not to sit too close to him. He seemed in a bad mood and I didn't want him lunging at me. He looked impatient and I detected a scowl that stretched from ear to ear. He made no effort to answer my questions about his speaking ability but did confide in me that he hated his owners (he wouldn't call them his parents) because they were vegetarians and wouldn't feed him tuna. "Look," he said, "where I come from, I had friends in the neighborhood who were getting chicken Purina and beef stew Whiskas. I felt inferior because of my diet. I felt like a pussy. The only protein I got was from garbage cans."

I tried to ignore the irony of him saying he felt like a pussy. He looked at me with such urgency that I couldn't look away—and I wanted to so badly, to see if there was some totally realistic hologram machine beaming this from somewhere. And then I started to think about petting Baxter and how it would never be the same. Or at least I wouldn't allow him to speak while I petted him. That would be too weird.

"Are you listening to me?" he asked heatedly. "The bitch has got to go."

I tried to snap my attention back to what he was actually saying. When he said bitch I thought he meant a female dog, but soon realized he was talking about my wife. "She's hardly here, and when she is she doesn't give me water or let me sleep in the cupboard like you do." He halted for a second and his voice became heavy with pain. "She even kicked me once,"—he bowed his head toward his crotch— "right here." He started mournfully licking the area she allegedly hurt. I didn't know it at the time, but Annie had kicked Baxter the week before, when she saw him peeing on my jacket.

I didn't know what to say. "I'm sorry," was all I could think of. He looked at me as if my apology was worth nothing.

"There's something else," he said then. "I hope you can trust my intuition about this." He pawed at the pillow pensively and then took a few steps toward me. "When Annie returned from her trip last month, she let me in and I slept on the couch with her after she unpacked her bags. I was next to her lap and I smelled something odd, something wrong." The phone rang at that moment, surprising both the cat and I. "Don't answer that," Baxter said. I knew it was Annie, calling to say good night. I leaned toward the phone and Baxter could see I was going to answer it. "God damn it," he muttered.

"Hello." It was Annie, as expected. "Nothing. Just getting ready for bed...uh huh...no, I'm just tired...I fell asleep watching TV." Baxter watched me sternly and shook his head. He was mouthing something to me but I couldn't figure it out. I listened to Annie on the other end as she talked about what she was working on. Baxter grew impatient. "Hang up," he said loudly.

"Who was that?" Annie asked.

"Nothing," I said. "I accidentally turned the TV up for a second."

"What are you watching?" she asked. She sounded a little mad.

"Something...about cats," I said. Baxter jumped off the couch and ran over to where the cordless phone was plugged in. He grabbed the wire with his front paws and started chewing on it. I thought about pushing him away from it. I knew I couldn't kick him. The phone line started to crackle. "I think the phone is running out of batteries," I said. Baxter stopped chewing and I was soon off the phone.

"You can't tell anybody about this. You understand?" he asked me.

I told him I understood but I wasn't sure if I really did. He said he had to go back home and that his owners were keeping closer tabs on him. "I think they know I come over here," he said. I asked him if he talked to anyone else, like his owners. "They couldn't handle it," he said. "They'd probably ask me a bunch of stupid shit anyway."

I was about to ask him if Bubbles also talked but stopped halfway. I suddenly felt very self-conscious. Baxter must have known what I wanted to ask. "My sister hasn't talked for two years," he said. "She used to talk to this boy in our old neighborhood. He was in a wheelchair and she felt sorry for him. But he tried to use her for sexual things once and she just clammed up. I've given up trying to talk to her." This story gave me an uncomfortable feeling that made me hum introspectively. Baxter went to the door and let out a couple of soft meows. His cat sounds alarmed me for some reason and made me think I was waking up from a dream. I stared at him wondering if he was even a real cat.

"Hey," he yelled sharply. "That means let me out."

I couldn't concentrate on anything the following day. I called in to the office and told them I was working at home. Instead I spent three hours Googling "talking cats" to see if there was any factual documentation of such a thing. Around lunchtime, as I made myself a ham sandwich, I heard Baxter's bell outside, clanging on the water bowl as he drank. I opened the door for him. "Hey," I said.

He came in and waited for me to shut the door. He seemed tired. "Got any of that tuna?" he asked. I opened the fridge and told him we did. "I need some," he said. I thought he was being a bit pushy but at the same time it was kind of cute. I put some on his plate. "I started digging last night," he said as he chewed.

"Digging for what?" I asked.

"Look in here," he said. He walked over to the low cupboard and nudged the door open. "There's a hole in the corner of your cupboard. And there's a hole in our cupboard, on the other side. There's a small tunnel connecting the two but it's too small for me. In a couple more nights though, I should have a nice passageway."

I looked into the cupboard and saw the square opening, about the size of a postcard. All I could say was "Wow. Okay."

Baxter narrowed his eyes at me and gave me a look that could have been a smile. "This way I can come over whenever I want to. I could eat your chicken scraps and sleep in your bed."

"Wait a minute," I said. "What's this about? Are you like, gay or something?"

He scoffed and took another bite of tuna. "There's no such thing as gay cats," he said. "Maybe bisexual, but not all the way gay." He walked over to me and started clawing at my shoes. "Oh yeah, that feels good."

"Why are you doing this?" I asked him.

He flipped over and closed his eyes as if he was going to fall asleep there on the kitchen floor. He waited a long pause before turning his head to look at me. "Look. This hurts me. I tried to tell you the other night. It's just, I know you can do better. That bitch of yours—all bitches really—are no good. Women are crazy. It's a proven fact. They don't have the right balance of chemicals. My first owner was a woman *and* a doctor and that's what she told all her patients."

"Why aren't you with her anymore?"

"I ran away. My sister too. We both ran away. But don't think we have it any better now. That old lady we live with never changes our litter box and then she gets mad at us when it starts to stink."

*creamy bullets*

I started to realize how ridiculous it was to be having this conversation. "Annie's not crazy," I said. "She's my wife and if you don't like it then you shouldn't hang out over here, and you shouldn't be digging a tunnel."

The next two nights, before Annie returned from her assignment, I could hear the faint, cautious sounds of Baxter digging and scratching somewhere in the kitchen wall, close to my cupboards. Once, late at night, I heard the old lady owner call for him and he had to stop digging. He must have been close because I heard him swear and scuttle back into his own cupboard. "There you are," I heard her voice say as he slinked out of her cupboard. "What were you doing in there?" she asked. But of course, he didn't answer.

Annie came home that weekend, lightly tanned, upbeat, and horny. We had sex twice on the first day upon her return. The second time was right after dinner and I could hear Baxter scratching closer and closer to his destination as Annie moved above me. Our bed squeaked and tapped the wall with our rhythm. I wondered if he could hear us and was getting angry. I started to fear an ambush by him. Maybe he snapped and was going to tell Annie about our talks. From the kitchen, I heard a sound. A soft hiccup like a baby crying. Annie jumped off of me, startled. "What's that sound? Is someone in our apartment?"

We put on our shirts and shorts and went into the kitchen. I heard Baxter mewing in our cupboard. "Is that Mr. Hoo-Ha?" asked Annie. I opened the door of the cupboard slowly and saw Baxter's head sticking out of the hole in the corner.

"I'm stuck," he whispered to me. He was able to make it sound like a hiss.

"How long has he been in there?" asked Annie. She was trying to see over my shoulders, past the pots and pans.

"I think there's a tunnel or passageway that he's found. But it looks like he can't quite fit."

"Aw," cooed Annie. "He must really love us."

I stuck my head further in and pushed him back from the opening. "I could probably cut this hole a little bigger so he could fit," I said to Annie. Baxter stuck his head back through the square and mewed a little more loudly, playing up his predicament. I heard the neighbor lady rustling around in her kitchen. She was opening her cupboards. I heard her make a sound like she was calling her cats. Dinner time. Baxter didn't make a sound but I could tell his head was full of swear words.

"Maybe we should go next door and tell her," Annie said quietly.

"No!" I said a little too sharply.

"Okay. Alright," said Annie. "Let me look for something to use."

"Finally, bitch," said Baxter.

Annie turned and froze. "What did you say to me?"

"I was talking to myself," I started. "I mean, I was talking to Mr. Hoo—um, Baxter. He tried to scratch me."

"It sounded like you were talking to me," she said.

"I was," said Baxter. But this time, I was looking at Annie when he spoke and she saw that my mouth didn't move.

Her eyes looked like they imploded in her head and she crouched down quickly and pushed me out of the way. "Who's in there?" she said into the cupboard. Baxter stared right at her and didn't say anything. I heard her voice soften a little as she started whispering to Baxter. The old lady next door dropped something in her kitchen and we all heard a great clang and crash. I tried to hear what Annie was saying. It sounded like baby talk. Annie's knees scooted back on the tiled floor and it looked like she was pulling on something. I was thinking about how dirty the floor was when she carefully withdrew from the cupboard, Baxter in her outstretched hands. He sneezed.

The next morning, after the neighbors left, I took my pocketknife and made the hole in our cupboard bigger so that Baxter could come and go more easily.

Whenever we made anything in the kitchen, he'd make his way over to see what we were cooking. He rolled around on the kitchen floor, getting the dust off his fur. Around midnight, he'd come by to sleep with us. He didn't speak when Annie was around and only tolerated her when she was, sometimes biting and scratching her extra hard when she tried to play with him. I was always nervous when he was around and I found myself not cuddling or kissing with Annie as much as I did before. I expected him to speak at any moment, especially those decreasing times when I showed affection to Annie.

Three weeks after I cut the hole in the cupboard bigger, the apartment manager stopped by. She'd received a call from the neighbor about the hole in their cupboard. After inspecting it, she found the tunnel that Baxter dug leading to our kitchen. She wanted to see if the tunnel ended in our kitchen somewhere. Baxter was actually sleeping on our bed at that very moment. Annie was at the grocery store.

The apartment manager opened all of our cabinets and pulled out her flashlight. She paused when she spotted the hole. I felt a rush of heat go through my body, like a liar who's been found out. "Do you see anything?" I asked.

She took out her cell phone. I thought she was going to call the police but she pushed a button and took a photograph. She stood up with the phone still unfolded in her hand. "Is their cat in here right now?" she asked me.

"I don't think so," I said. I wanted her to leave but I wasn't sure if I had the right to kick her out since she was the manager. I heard Baxter's bell ring in the bedroom, as if he was getting up.

"What's that?" she asked.

"That's our phone," I said unconvincingly.

She exhaled out of her nostrils like she was trying not to laugh. "That's all I need," she said.

Two days later, we got an eviction notice in the mail.

As we loaded up the U-Haul, the old neighbors took turns watching us through their kitchen window. Baxter was nowhere to be seen but Bubbles paced around casually, sometimes stopping to look into a tree for birds or squirrels. Annie and I both felt numb, confused, and ashamed. I told her that I had gone down to the office and talked about the hole. But I didn't. My mouth was hard and heavy like concrete.

We had found a place that was a little smaller and cheaper on the other side of town. No cats were allowed. All the apartments that allowed cats smelled badly. We still didn't have time for a pet anyway.

I closed the back of the U-Haul and got in the driver's side. Annie sat in the passenger seat, taking a last look around. Her eyes looked glassy and out of focus, as if she were having a panic attack. Her neck was tense and straight. I could tell that she was looking for Baxter. As I started the engine, I looked over to the neighbors' window and saw them both standing there, framed by their drawn curtains and raised blinds. The old man held Baxter in his arms with a look on his face that said, *See who he loves?* One of Baxter's white legs dangled awkwardly and I could see him starting to squirm. The man, his "dad" as we had called him, struggled to hold the cat in his arms. I could tell he was determined to hold Baxter like that until we drove off. Annie saw this too, and we both bluntly stared, our heads turned ninety degrees. I reached over and grabbed Annie's hand. The old lady reached for the blinds and started lowering them. They came down smoothly, silently, like a guillotine.

# Jealousy is Policy

There's the girl who loves chocolate and eats nothing but cake. She eats her lunch in the shack, outside by the recycling bins. We can never find her when a customer comes for her. Sometimes the customers get mad and kick over tables.

Whenever I eat in the back room, I keep an eye on the shack. I can see it through the windows. I eat grilled chicken and potatoes in the back room. The other girls come back and get jealous of my chicken. The smell is so good and strong and it sticks to the walls in the back room for the whole day.

No one else is happy here.

Once we caught Stacey, a frumpish woman in her late 30's, trying to microwave a fork in the back room. We scolded her and wrote a memo about things not to put in the microwave, and the next day she was dead.

June is the one who eats her lunch in the shack. Her mouth is always covered in chocolate residue when she's working. The customers seem to like it but we always make fun of her. Some say that she lives in a fort by the water, that she is the daughter of a boatman. They say the boatman is always calling her on his boat phone. What is a boat phone?

There's an attractive janitor that cleans the floors at night. I can't believe he's not a model. If you took pictures of him and hung them up in a store window, people would start walking in, I'm sure. He always makes sure that all of us girls get in our cars at night before he starts cleaning the floors. He has a tattoo on his hand. I wonder what he eats for lunch.

"That chicken—," they say to me, but they never finish. I'm convinced that they are just jealous.

Sometimes June, the chocolate girl, makes something for everyone. Once she made a pan of brownies with peanut butter in the middle. She says she can't live without chocolate. Once, Kimberly said something about how June was going to "overdose on chocolate," but we thought it was so stupid, what Kimberly said. Kimberly was someone who made more money than all of us put together.

Of course it didn't take long for my boss to say something about the chicken. "If that's all you're going to eat," she said, "you can eat it in the shack, where we don't have to watch you." Plus she said I wasn't working hard enough, that I needed to ask for help when I was having problems with a customer. Customers were complaining about me and also my clothes, she said. My boss was the type of person who liked to pop pimples on us whenever the opportunity arose.

Later that same day a photographer came to take pictures of us for a newspaper story. It was an old lady in her 70's and we all made fun of her behind her back. She told me I had pretty hands.

There was a rumor going around that Janet and Lori planned to burn down the shack while June and I were in there eating lunch. The shack started smelling more and more sickly—like moldy eggs—and I was scared of its history. "It just showed up one day," said Jack, the quiet old man who actually owned our building. "I expected someone to come back and get it, tow it away on a trailer, but it has stayed there for a long time. And there are tools in it," he said. "And pictures on the wall."

June and I discussed the pictures in there as we ate lunch. She liked them and wanted to bring them home to hang in her living room. They made me feel uneasy, all these close-up photos of people's eyes and noses.

"I like caramel best with chocolate, see this?" June held up a thin bar of chocolate and dumped a spoonful of caramel from a jar on top. It oozed over the sides and June giggled as she opened her mouth largely.

"Can I try it?" I asked. She chewed and shifted the glob in her mouth, her cheeks bulging. "Jesus," I said, laughing. There was a line of caramel hanging from her chin.

She finally swallowed and said, "I can stick my whole fist in my mouth." She opened her mouth and showed me. I scooted near her and looked at her arm going into her mouth. I shook my head and she took out her hand and wiped it off on her shirt. She grabbed the spoon and prepared a piece for me.

"What do you think these pictures mean?" I asked June.

"I think they mean: a good place to eat chicken and chocolate."

Soon after that there was a memo that told everyone June was no longer going to work with us, but instead, she'd only work in the shack, preparing signs and making equipment for the rest of us. Whenever the boatman called for her we had to crinkle paper in the receiver and tell him that we couldn't hear him, that the line was bad, that he had to use a regular phone. One night a man came in and started crying like a baby. We didn't know who he was, but some say it was the boatman. He cried with great drama and said nothing in any discernible language. Private Nurse Nancy had to take him outside and give him aspirin and a map. She walked with him to the corner and he was never seen again. The next day the boatman called and was angry and loud and said with much anger: "Don't you know this water is getting godamned cold. Godamn you all to Hell and I hope you never board a ship on my river. For the waves will rise and crash upon you like an angry hammer from the Mother Nature. When I think of all of you there in that place, I laugh until I can't breathe, I get sick to my throat and I spit on the dangerous jagged rocks of my shore. All of you, animals without a soul."

I was then told not to eat out there in the shack again or to deliver any memos to her. She did not want to be disturbed, the boss told me. "She is making something in there that will be a surprise to you," the boss said.

When the newspaper article and the photographs appeared it caused quite a stir. A famous movie producer visited us and was satisfied with the service he received. He wanted to make our little group into a movie, he said. I don't think he knew anything about June or the way we all hated each other or the way I ate chicken in the back room. "I want to show the world your strength," he told us later at a teleconference. But we were suspicious. Even the man who cleans our floors at night said, "How could he make a movie about you twits? All you do is complain and throw stuff on the floor." Kimberly said he was just resentful. When she first started working here, Kimberly had an intimate moment with the janitor, reportedly on a desk somewhere, and so we all assumed she knew what his every thought and emotion was.

Of course, months later, the famous producer stopped writing letters and no one but our regular customers cared about our outstanding services. There was much work to be performed and we completed each task like our lives depended on it.

At just about the time our morale was getting dangerously low, a wonderful thing happened. I was in the back room eating grilled chicken and potatoes when I noticed the shack was gone. A rainbow-colored van drove up to the back door where the shack used to be and I almost started crying. The tears that were climbing to my eyes stopped at my throat. I swallowed and stood up. The old lady who took photographs of us months beforehand got out of the driver's side of the van and walked to the back doors of the vehicle. I watched her as she strong-armed a trio of dark brown figures, each of which was about the size of a statue you'd find on someone's front lawn. The figures were of hunched-over old women and each had a silly grin on their chiseled faces. My heart squeezed itself when I realized the statues were made from chocolate. The old lady looked at me and nodded before climbing back into the driver's seat and making the odd vehicle cough its way away.

I went outside and looked at each statue, wondering if June had made them, and also wondering if they were hollow. If they were hollow they might crumble in my hands. I could just see everyone laughing at me if I tried to move the things and they broke all over me. It was cool outside but the sun was bright and mean. A bead of chocolate sweat ran down one of the wrinkled-looking faces.

I decided not to tell anyone about the chocolate. Someone else would come into the back room and see the statues through the windows. They would call for help. Someone else would know exactly what to do. I went back inside and turned my chair around so I couldn't see them. I finished my potatoes and sniffed the air for the stench of my half-eaten chicken. I sweated and prayed for someone else to come into the back room. Sometimes customers would ask for me but when I went out to the main room they would wave me back to the back room. I averted my eyes, not wanting to display responsibility for the things outside. I heard a man raising his voice to the other girls working. Then Janet and Lori could be heard laughing. I tried to eat but couldn't.

I felt lonely and jealous.

# Close Your Eyes

At night, she grabs a pair of binoculars and looks out her upstairs window. She sees a boy, not far away, taking his clothes off in a blue bedroom. She holds her breath and watches for a minute. When the boy pulls down on his underwear, she looks away. Then she puts on a worn-out leather jacket and goes for a walk around the neighborhood.

She walks by the boy's house and wonders if she may see something that the boy owns or plays with. A ball or possibly a bike, (if he's old enough maybe a car). She sees a toy gun and imagines him holding it. She is close enough to breathe on it. She can feel its presence in her field of vision. She puts her hands in her pockets and whistles. She is alarmed by how loud it sounds.

From here, she walks to the grocery store to buy something sweet (candy bars are cheap). She smiles at the clerk and thinks of the boy undressing in the window. When the clerk says "Thank you", she says "Window".

She goes back home and looks out the window again. She sees the boy's feet at the foot of his bed and some dirty underwear nearby. Socks can also be seen; they look pink or red. She can tell that the boy has walked around the house for quite a while before taking them off. They are filthy. She closes her eyes and swallows her sweet treat. She keeps swallowing and breathing heavier.

Next, she has in her hand the top of a spray paint can. It is a red plastic lid. She wiggles it between her legs and manages to hold it tightly inside of her. The man who picks up her recyclable plastic on Monday morning is positioned over her. They struggle for a minute until he has his wide penis stuffed full inside the lid. She points to her mouth but doesn't say a word. He stands up and quietly puts his pants on. Then, she wakes up.

She laughs at herself, and then goes about her day.


In the afternoon paper she reads a story about two missing women (thought dead in the snowy mountains) being discovered alive in a cave after seven days. There is a picture of them drinking juice on plastic chairs in a hospital somewhere. She wonders if they had sex with each other as they waited to die in the cave. It was two men who found the women. Their names are Joe and Larry; she doesn't bother to picture what they look like. Wondering about women seems so much easier than wondering about men. "Men are predictable," she says to herself. She talks to herself while reading the paper often.

She folds the newspaper up and takes a cup of tea out to the front porch. She sits and watches six teen-agers across the street playing basketball. She quickly notices that one of them is the boy she saw partially undress the night before. She watches only him, and after a few minutes pass, he seems to notice this and starts moving like someone who is self-conscious of being watched. She hears two of the boys talking but the one she watches does not say anything while they discuss a girl at school.

"How was Rachel last night? You get any?"

"Shit, boy. You know I did. I busted her last year when we were playing Truth-or-Dare at Jenny's house."

"Oh man, Jenny's one I'd like to jump on. She's got that big ass and stuff."

"Those big lips have gotta be good for more than just playing flute."

*creamy bullets*

She sees the boy smile in a clumsy uncomfortable way because of this comment. Then she realizes that the boy is smiling at her. She averts her eyes and then looks back to see that the boy is looking at the roof of her house, as if trying to find the window.

That night she watches again as the boy walks around his blue room looking for something, or so it seems. He leaves her view for a few minutes and then returns to be seen in the window frame. He has a suitcase that he is packing.

She watches with the upstairs lights turned off and a bowl of salad at her side. The binoculars are around her neck and used only to see random details. She watches for so long on this night that she actually stops a few times to pull the phone nearby and call friends. The boy slowly packs the suitcase with all his clothes still on. She talks into the telephone about books, politics, and a brother who is a doctor.

The boy is staying up late. But around three o' clock in the morning he finally begins to undress. She sees through the binoculars that his belly button sticks out like a balloon knot, but his chest is near perfect in a lifeguard kind of way. She guesses that he is sixteen and maybe started lifting weights at fifteen. He drinks milk, she notices. He does not remove his underwear tonight, but instead he again starts moving about as if he knows he is being watched. After fidgeting with a Velcro wallet and an alarm clock he gets in bed and the lights go out.

She watches TV for an hour and tries to masturbate while watching a TV movie, but does not find it as easy as usual. She falls asleep on the couch at 4:20.


At 9:00 that morning she is awaken by the telephone.

"I don't want you watching me anymore," a man on the line says.

After a moment of shocked silence she says: "Who is this?"

"I'm running away. I've got other things I can do. Another place to live. I'm not just a freak all the time. You know that, don't you?" The voice sounds younger as he talks. It starts to shake at the end of the sentences.

She sits up and turns the TV off. "Do you live on 17th street?" she asks.

"Right next to you. You watched us playing basketball yesterday."

"I'm sorry, I shouldn't have been doing that, in the window I mean."

"I have to tell you something about those boys you saw me with. They don't like you. I have to come over and tell you some things. Like, they've done stuff to me." The boy's voice is clipped and tough.

◄ *creamy bullets*

When she wakes up again, it is 11:45 and the boy has not come over to talk as he said he would. She wonders if it was really him on the phone. That day, she goes to a bagel shop and writes letters, then goes to a record store and allows herself to buy two cassettes. When she comes home at 7:00, there is no sign that the boy has been there. There is a notepad that she has taped to the front door but no messages have been left.

At 3:00 in the morning, she is awakened by the doorbell. It rings two times before she realizes she is not dreaming this. She gets up and is putting on clothes as the doorbell rings a third time, and then the sound of someone kicking the door. She goes downstairs and looks through the window by the front door but nobody is there. She goes to her kitchen and looks out the side window and sees the boy quietly climbing onto the roof of his house. She wants to say something to him but is still unsure if it was really him that called her the day before. She goes back upstairs preparing to say something to him through the window, but when she gets there he is already in his room.

His bedroom is lighted by one candle. He moves slowly and catlike around the room, stuffing some things into a backpack. She watches, as always, in the dark. He sheds the clothes from his small, tight body. This time he is wearing girls' underwear. She does not look away. He pulls down on the elastic and his cock tumbles out, looking bigger than it should on his young body. She grabs her binoculars to see closer. His ass fills the magnified scope. His naked body turns twice as he looks for something in his room (his hands are opened in confused gesture). He leaves her view for a second before returning with a chair. He sits naked in the chair, and faces, as if staring, toward her with his legs crossed. She feels warm and sad inside, like a best friend is telling her a deep secret.

There is no movement between them for several minutes. He cannot see her until she reaches above her and pulls a string. Now she is lighted and he sees her wearing a loose T-shirt and boxer shorts, sitting on her wooden floor. He looks down and uncrosses his legs. His cock hangs down, long and half-hard. She focuses her binoculars on a small pinkish-blue vagina, also between his legs.

The light in his room flickers dimmer, and fades to nothing.

In the morning, a police car is parked in front of her house. A policewoman is talking to her neighbors, who appear to be distressed about something. When

*creamy bullets*

she steps outside to get the newspaper another policewoman asks her if she's seen her neighbor, the young boy, who hasn't been home since the previous morning, they say. She tells them no, but is nervous and goes back inside.

The window shades are closed and she sits in her rocking chair watching the silhouettes of the police and neighbors on the sidewalk. They motion toward the other boys' houses across the street. They point at his bedroom window on the side of the house. Once they leave, she remains in the rocking chair, thinking about the boy, with the newspaper in her lap.

In the Metro section of the paper, she reads an article about a dog who was run over by its own master. There is a photograph of the car.

When the day turns to night, she looks out the window, the action now a habit. It is still dark. She decides to walk to the store. At the store she buys ketchup, a steak knife, and a cheap magazine with a picture of a comedian on it. The man at the cash register does not say Thank You.

Outside the store, a tall pimply boy from her street asks her to buy beer for him and his friends. She turns around and sees four boys sitting in a big car. She remembers watching them play basketball the other day. The pimply boy holds out a twenty dollar bill. He is sweating badly. She looks at the other boys. They, too, seem sweaty. One of them opens a car door. The sound is loud in the empty, litter-strewn parking lot. The pimply boy seems to pull his hand back and step toward her aggressively. She hears the sound of boots stepping onto pavement. She clutches her bag tightly, almost cutting her hand on the knife inside. "You can keep the change," the pimply boy says quietly out of the side of his mouth. The twenty drops out of his fingers and onto the ground. She looks at the boys in the car. They are smiling now.

"You want to go drink with us?" asks the boy wearing boots. Someone in the car is laughing. She grabs the money off the ground and gives it back to the pimply boy, who seems to be standing too close to her.

"I don't have my license with me," she says, "otherwise I would." The booted boy begins to kick the side of the car.

"We'll give you a drive home so you can get your license," says the boy in the driver's seat. She notices that he is wearing sunglasses. The boy in the passenger seat also has dark glasses and a stocking cap pulled tight over his head.

"I have to go," she says, but the sound of three car doors opening overtake her words. She runs around the corner of the building and flees down a wide alley. Dogs begin to bark when she knocks over a garbage can full of glass. The palm of her hand bleeds. She hides behind someone's wooden fence, in a dark backyard. The boys can be heard, calling out to her from the alley's edge. One of them is throwing rocks, hitting cars. She waits for silence, and then starts back down the alley in the direction of her house.

The moon is half-full and casts a pale glow at the end of the alley. As she gets closer she sees a wooden chair by her fence. It is empty; but also nearby is a package of some sort. When she gets closer she sees that it is a sleeping bag. It is zipped up, and there is something inside it. She kicks it lightly with her foot. Then, bending down, she starts to unzip it.

When she sees the head seemingly lunge toward her, she almost screams. It is the neighbor boy inside the bag. She pulls back the flap and sees that the body is twitching and the boy's mouth is searching for air, opening and closing like teeth chattering. "What—" she says quietly, but stops short, too scared to make a sound. His arms grab weakly, blindly, at her arms. She starts to pull him up, out of the sleeping bag, but drops him suddenly. Her legs are like liquid, now that she sees the blood between his legs. He has been cut and she notices dark blue pieces of skin where his penis had been. The vagina is more red and swollen than when she saw it before.

She falls to her knees and holds the boy close. She hears his breathing. Or maybe it's the night breeze playing with her ear. His touch is cold and still. Her face is against his. Their lips, tongues, teeth. Their blood.

"Close your eyes," she says. She closes his eyes. "Just go," she says. Her fingers in his mouth. "Don't—"...She looks at his house and up at his window, all of it dark. Music is heard all of a sudden, slowly increasing in volume. She looks down the alley, but it's still dark. His mouth falls open and his tongue stretches out of it. She presses her mouth against the tongue, sucks it between her teeth. She bites on the tough outer skin. She feels her teeth meet, the boy's tongue filling her mouth. Then it all comes loose.

# Dirtclod Season

"I'll make your life hell! Now give me $75!"

I obviously had no choice, so I gave Dee the $75. She was leaving me for someone else and had decided to hate my guts. She knew where I lived and knew I had a reputation for being considerate.

"If you don't give me $75, I won't give back the keys to your apartment," she demanded. I pulled out my wallet.

"I don't want to see you again," she said, shaking the money in my face. "I don't need you anymore."

For the next week I stayed in bed and cried. I stared at the ceiling and let the tears roll down into my ears. I wept so much I got an ear infection.

I was going out with a girl who was three inches taller than me. The week before I started dating her, I stood behind her at a rock concert. She was wearing a camisole and a short lacy skirt and I stared at her exquisite brown shoulders all night, wanting to grab her and bite her like a vampire. Later that night she pinned me against a cigarette machine and gave me her phone number. Her name was Montana.

Our first date was at her work. She worked the graveyard shift alone at a video dubbing company. She told me about her impulsive freewheeling life style and her alternative rock band that played at Jewish weddings, bar mitzvahs and benefits for local politicians.

I helped her load 200 machines full of videotapes and by that time we were ready for intimacy. She showed me a spacious control room with nice carpet where we laid down together. "We have 38 minutes before this tape is done," she warned me.

During oral sex, it became apparent to me that she was very hard to please. She was very specific on where to position my mouth and it usually took a good 20 minutes of steady rhythm to bring her to climax. My jaw often felt sore or broken the next morning.

*creamy bullets*

## — ON BEING PAID TO DRINK —

I visited Montana many nights when she worked. Some nights we spent time in the darkened control room and other nights we went to a bar down the street where we watched the minutes tick by and drank bottles of beer. When we played pool I could see the competitiveness and pride pulsing through her body. She'd walk with a toughened stride.

All the men in the bar would look at her and feel her presence in the room. She was too beautiful, too loud, too tall. I wondered how many people shook their dizzy heads whenever I would slap her ass playfully. We'd plug the jukebox full of 80's hits and leave the bar whenever it was time to go back to change video tapes.

At first I was worried that she would get caught taking these little beer breaks but she told me, "Don't worry about it. Everybody else is sleeping."

## — ON MEMORY —

I often told myself: I could really use that $75 right now. I knew that Dee was seeing someone else and that she probably hustled him for money too. I thought about all the times she swindled money from my wallet, mostly for drugs or Taco Bell. She had a thing for junk, in all its various guises.

The fact that I left a rewarding 5-year relationship with my previous girlfriend to pursue something with Dee makes the memories even more baffling. My penis had sabotaged my life.

Easily the most inconsiderate girlfriend I ever had, I felt the repercussions of Dee even after I began seeing Montana. I realized that she had even infected my brain with evil thoughts and unneeded images of her past, which she candidly and brutally told me about. Unspeakable things about various diseases that she had carried and her sexual escapades with gutter punks.

At the height of my despair, just before I went to the doctor for my ear infection, I ran into a busy street and rolled over the top of a new Lexus. Somehow I managed to walk away from that incident with a scrape on my right hand and my emotional state more dead than ever. Some times I lashed out at Montana for no good reason and I couldn't understand why. Then she'd get pissed at me and go down to the bar without me.

The worst thing that Dee ever said to me was: "I don't really care what you do or think."

— ON MY REASONS —

I thought it was important for Montana to know about the short turbulent relationship I shared with Dee.

It was always hard for me to tell the story without making it sound like I was bitter or like Dee was a spoiled unreasonable bitch. I was, and she was. Some times Montana had a hard time believing some of my stories about Dee. She'd look angry, shocked, or jealous. I'd want to throw up my hands and just say, "Everyone's guilty."

"It sounds like a soap opera," she'd say, chewing on nachos and slurping beer.

## — ON FIGHTING —

I've been in one fight during my lifetime. It was when I was in fifth grade and the only thing I remember was my sister whispering in my ear to "get him in the nuts" or something to that effect. The fight was soon over and we walked home.

I don't remember my sister ever getting in a fight, but if she did I wouldn't know what to tell her, seeing as her opponent would probably be lacking "nuts."

Girl fights in general, however, are often much more exciting than guy fights. With guys it's like their limbs are all wound up and when they start wailing away it's like a cartoon or something; just a cloud of dust and Bam! and Pow! Girls usually move a little slower so the action is easier to analyze. Whoever coined the term "cat fight" is not being realistic. Cats are also like cartoons, rolling around in a ball of hyper slashes and hisses. Girls fight more like elk, locking horns and swaying, rarely falling to the ground. You'll see an occasional swing but those are often thrown in an apish windmill style that is easy to see coming.

## — ON IDEAS OF REVENGE —

One night while I was out with Montana, in the midst of my forced smiles, stiff drinks and sloppy pool shooting I came up with a brilliant idea. An idea that would make new memories; ones that would replace the ugly ones; ones that would make me sleep easier at night knowing that I was with the right person and I deserved to be happy.

I told Montana that the whole idea relied on her participation. "Let's go over to Dee's house so you can kick her ass in her front yard," I said.

Montana looked at me over her drink and said, "That's a good idea." We had another drink for luck before driving over to Dee's. We drove in silence for a moment before Montana asked how we were going to start it.

"I thought you would just call her out and tell her who you are. I'm sure you won't need my help." I had thought of this beforehand and realized it was a pretty even match, both girls being psychotic and hyper. Two separate incidents helped me foresee the outcome: Dee had once been kicked out of a bar for taking her shirt off and dancing on a pool table. Montana had once been kicked out of the same place for standing on the bar and kicking a guy's beer across the room.

"What's in this for me?" she asked as we pulled over in front of the house.

"A never-ending legend, street credibility, a fearful sense of respect from others, renewed faith in your fists, and possibly $75."

Her eyes lit up a little at the $75 part and then she began muttering, "Spoiled brat bitch, stripper slut coke whore…"

— ON ACTIONS, REACTIONS, OUTCOMES —

We got out of the car and the porch light came on. It was one o'clock in the morning and the only sound in the neighborhood was the clicking of several sprinklers. I never understood how Dee and her older sister could afford rent on a house in a nice neighborhood.

Before we got to the door, it creaked open and Dee stepped out in pajama bottoms and a T-shirt. She looked at Montana and then saw me standing by the car. Montana stepped forward and hit her in the face with a hard fist. Dee stumbled back before catching herself on the doorknob. Montana grabbed her other arm and tried swinging her into the front yard. Dee reached up and grabbed a handful of Montana's hair, but since Montana was a good six inches taller than her she quickly jabbed Dee in the ribs and loosened her grasp. Montana stepped back and flung her fist again, but this time only connected with Dee's shoulder and neck.

As Montana was rearing back to deliver a kick, her older sister came out on the porch and told us that she had called the police. Montana backed away and came back over to the car.

We sped away and drove a few blocks before the car started sputtering and broke down. We parked it in a hospital parking lot and decided to walk the remaining couple of miles. I felt like shouting loudly but Montana still seemed kind of tense. I picked various flowers for her along the sidewalk and began making a bouquet. "It seems like you hate both of us," she finally said. "Why would you make me do that?"

"I don't know," I said, stopping to think. "I guess love makes you do crazy things."

She shook her head. "You don't love me," she said.

"You're right," I said. "But who knows." I handed her the makeshift flower arrangement.

"You don't know. You don't know shit," she said. "Somebody else loved you and then hurt you and

*creamy bullets*

now you'll always want revenge. At least until you decide to deal with it another way." She looked at the flowers, an effortless gift, stolen sentiment. She dropped them and walked ahead of me.

I knew then that this relationship was all but over. I had plenty of things to think about and fix with myself. I tried to think of things that would give my life balance, a clear clean vision. I knew I couldn't dwell on the past and create enemies out of assumptions. I saw a row of tall sunflowers and I leaned over the fence to pull one out of the ground. I saw Montana walking away and I wanted to tell her that I was sorry, that I admired her for what she did.

I ran to catch up and stopped a good distance from her. "Hey Montana," I called to her. She turned around and I pitched the flower toward her like a softball. She took a step toward me, not seeing clearly in the dark. That is when the roots and the clump of dirt clustered to them flew into her surprised face.

"Why did you do that?" she asked. I stood there like an idiot. My enthusiasm was being turned on and off all night. I was worn out. "WHY DID YOU DO THAT!" she yelled. A few porch lights came on and I could sense that people were watching us through their windows, angry and sleepy. "Why did you—" She stopped herself and began quickly walking away from me. I turned around and decided to go back to my car, broken down in the hospital lot. I would sleep in the backseat until something woke me up.

All the porch lights switched back off. I looked for the moon but couldn't find it. I was in the dark, alone.

KEVIN SAMPSELL lives in Portland, Oregon. He has run the influential micropress, Future Tense Books, since 1990. His short fiction, criticism, and essays have appeared widely. He is also the editor of *The Insomniac Reader* (Manic D Press) and the author of *Beautiful Blemish* (Word Riot Press).

9 780981 502731